*LARGE*
PRINT

# KILLER BROTHERS

Ben Gleason, nearing the end of a long prison sentence for killing his father's murderer, is told that his younger brother has been sentenced to hang in five days' time. In a desperate attempt to save his brother, Ben escapes and starts the long journey home. He faces danger and temptation before his journey ends in a tragic discovery. Instead of being reunited with his family and the woman he hoped to marry, Ben experiences a living nightmare. Soon, he may well face the hangman's noose himself.

BILL WILLIAMS

# KILLER BROTHERS

*Complete and Unabridged*

# LINFORD
*Leicester*

First published in Great Britain in 2004 by
Robert Hale Limited
London

First Linford Edition
published 2005
by arrangement with
Robert Hale Limited
London

The moral right of the author has been asserted

British Library CIP Data

Williams, Bill, *1940 –*
    Killer brothers.—Large print ed.—
Linford western library
1. Western stories
2. Large type books
I. Title
823.9'2 [F]

ISBN 1–84617–017–6

Published by
F. A. Thorpe (Publishing)
Anstey, Leicestershire

Set by Words & Graphics Ltd.
Anstey, Leicestershire
Printed and bound in Great Britain by
T. J. International Ltd., Padstow, Cornwall

This book is printed on acid-free paper

# 1

A fellow prisoner, newly arrived, gave Ben Gleason the grim news. His brother, Lyle Gleason, was scheduled to hang on 7 June 1879, just five days from now. He was being held at the jail in Arberstown, Ben's hometown. Ben was overwhelmed with guilt, feeling he was to blame. It might have been different if he had been home instead of being in prison himself. His mother would be devastated and now he should be at home with her. Perhaps he had a chance of getting early release because of the special circumstances. With just three months to serve, the state authorities might show compassion and grant him parole.

Lucas Callow, the chief guard at the Cragoma Plains state prison, sounded encouraging at first and told him to put his request in writing, which he did.

Callow promised to pass on the request, but he had no intention of doing so. He had smiled when he told Ben that it had been turned down.

Shortly afterwards, Ben realized that he only had one option and that was to try and escape, and damn the consequences. He would need help and he knew the man who could provide it, but it wouldn't come cheap.

Ben drew heavily on what would be his last cigarette as he waited for Zak Crowe to meet him in the exercise yard. He hoped that his supply of cigarettes, an assortment of books, fifty-five dollars and a fancy belt would be enough for Zak.

The appearance of the two men who had been in prison for almost the same time couldn't have been more contrasting. Ben's twenty-five-year-old frame was thin and the face hidden beneath the shaggy beard was gaunt. The pale-blue eyes held a frightened look where they had once been smiling and soft. The rotund Zak Crowe looked as though he didn't have a care in the world, clearly enjoying the prospect of more business that would make sure that when he left prison he would have a bankroll that would help set him up for something really big.

Ben had worked out his own plan. He explained that he intended to escape when he was outside the prison working with the logging-party. He would need a map and a horse by tomorrow.

Crowe gave a sharp intake of breath.

'Anything's possible, Gleason, but with such little notice it would probably cost you everything that you own plus that shirt on your back.'

Ben looked glum. 'I could arrange to get some money sent back to you.' He sensed that even before payment had been worked out he wasn't going to have enough.

'Sorry, Gleason but I don't do credit. Let's be honest, there's a good chance that Callow will put a bullet in your back tomorrow and then I'll be out of pocket with the people that I've made arrangements with. No, it's strictly payment in full. So what can you put up?'

Ben slowly listed his assets, trying to make them as impressive as possible but his hopes faded when he saw Zak shaking his head.

'It must be close on a hundred miles to where you're heading and you can just about afford a mule without a saddle.' Crowe paused to let the bad news register before he asked: 'Whatever happened to that nice gold ring that you had when you came in here. Did you sell it?'

Ben had hidden the chunky gold ring that had been given to him by his pa. He had already had one finger hacked off when he first arrived in prison and didn't fancy losing another one if someone tried to steal the ring. He had never thought he would ever part with it but he would have to let it go.

'Would we have a deal if I gave you the ring on the condition that you'll promise to sell it back to me one day if I pay you double what it's worth?'

Crowe's face broke into a smile. 'Sure, but the horse I get for you won't be any thoroughbred. You meet me after supper and hand over the goods, including the ring. I'll give you the map and tell you where you can pick up the horse. We'll work out a rough time.'

'And the horse will definitely be there?' Ben asked, realizing that it was a stupid question. He had no choice but to trust Zak Crowe.

Crowe offered Ben his hand. 'You've just secured yourself a horse, Gleason. My business could only survive on trust. I not only give you my word but I swear on my dear ma's life that the horse will be there. See you after supper.'

As Crowe walked away he shouted back to Ben: 'And if that horse ain't there then you come back and complain to me.'

Ben hoped that Crowe's laughter was only the result of his twisted sense of humour but he was fairly certain that Crowe had once told him that his mother was dead!

According to the prisoner who had brought the news, his brother Lyle had confessed to killing a man, making his death-sentence a formality even though he was only eighteen years old. Lyle was exactly the same age as Ben had been when he had shot the man who had killed his father. The judge had been lenient on Ben because of the circumstances, but he had paid for taking the law into his own hands. He didn't know what sort of man his brother had turned out to be but if he could save him from a hanging then he had to help him, even if it meant a longer stay in prison for himself or perhaps worse.

Ben finalised the deal with Crowe when they met up as arranged. The map that Crowe handed over was basic and probably not very accurate but the second part of the route followed the river so that would make things easier.

He just needed to get that quarter of mile to the horse and then he would have a chance.

★ ★ ★

When the working party left the prison the following day to make the two mile journey to the woods, Ben was filled with apprehension. The prison had been built on the edge of the plains and anyone escaping from the prison itself would have needed to travel a long way in open country before reaching any form of cover. There were just six prisoners in the party accompanied by Lucas Callow and they had been following the same routine for the past three months. All those in the party were coming to the end of their sentences and were deemed to be trusted with an axe. With Callow standing within rifle-range there wasn't much chance that a prisoner would use the axe as a weapon, except maybe to take a swipe at a fellow-inmate.

Ben was relieved to find that it was another very hot day because he planned to make a run for it when he was taking his 'rest' period under the shade of some trees. He had told his friend Denny Foley about his plans and Denny had agreed to keep watch in case Callow came snooping around the rest area. If that happened then Denny would do his best to distract him. If Callow stayed clear, Ben would have thirty minutes before the guard would discover that he had made a run for it and if he gave chase he would assume that Ben had headed directly towards Arberstown. But Ben had other ideas.

Ben attacked the fallen trees with extra vigour, trying to keep his thoughts off what he was going to do. It was getting close to the time for the rest period, when Foley nodded in the direction of the guard.

'Looks as if Zak Crowe is cooking up some sort of deal with Callow. I hope you can trust Crowe, Ben, because without that horse you'll be back inside by tonight and who knows what Callow will do to you.'

Ben had won more than his fair share of fights in prison against some big men but Callow was built like an ape and he thrived on inflicting pain on others. He would discard his weapon when punishing a prisoner, openly inviting him to pit himself against him, man to man, but Callow could have defeated three of them at a time, such was his strength and brutality.

Ben frowned when he saw Crowe and Callow looking over towards him. He had some concerns about Crowe but explained to his buddy:

'I don't really have any choice, Denny. Anyway it's too late now . . . ' He was interrupted by a shout from Callow telling him to take a break.

'*Adios*, Denny,' Ben whispered. 'I hope we meet again one day and thanks.'

'Good luck, Ben. I hope I don't see you too soon.'

If all went well, Foley knew that he

would miss his friend and that Callow would make all those left behind suffer in some way, but it would be worth it if it helped Ben.

Ben's tiredness from working in the hot sun soon evaporated as he slipped into the wooded area and started sprinting through the trees, praying that all would go well. He was panting hard and his leg-muscles ached by the time he reached the other side of the woods and the spot that he hoped was the meeting-point. It was the first time he had run since he had been in prison and although his upper-body strength was strong his lower limbs had lost a great deal of muscle over the years. He walked a short distance either side of the small rocks to make sure that there wasn't a similar spot nearby.

'Come on, where are you?' he said out loud. All the doubts about Zak flooded back. Five minutes later he was thinking what a fool he'd been. Zak could just tell him that his outside contact had let him down and wouldn't offer any refund of payment. The question was what to do next. He could return to the rest area and avoid a severe beating from Callow or he could take his chances on foot and hope he might get lucky and be able to get a horse from somewhere. Ben made his decision and started to run.

'Hey fella, don't you want this horse?' a voice called from behind him.

He stopped and turned to see a rider come out from the trees holding the reins of a black gelding. It took a second or two before Ben realized that it was the horse intended for him. He ran back.

The rider leaned down and offered him the reins.

'I hope you make it, fella, wherever it is you're heading. There's some food and drink in the bag. It's nothing special but probably better than you're used to.'

Ben offered the man his hand.

'Thanks buddy. Now I must get going.'

'Hang on. Crowe asked me to give you this.'

The man reached into his vest pocket and handed Ben his pa's gold ring.

'Crowe said that you weren't to tell anyone about this because he had his reputation to think of.'

Ben smiled, pleased that his fears about Crowe had been unfounded. He nudged his heels into the gelding and it responded with a burst of speed. It felt good to be back in the saddle but he cautioned himself not to push the animal too hard. There was no point in having a couple of days of hard riding and then have the horse break down. His plan was to head north for about ten miles and then pick up a trail that would take him west and to the start of the journey to Arberstown. When Ben reached the top of the hill he pulled on the reins and then turned to look in the direction of the prison. The rows of single storey wooden cell-blocks would have looked grim even in the bright sunshine but they were too far away to see. He doubted if he would ever rid his mind of the memories of the past seven years. At times it had been a living hell, thanks to Lucas Callow. Ben had been introduced to a new word when he had heard his cell mate whisper 'sadist' when Callow walked close to them one day.

Ben wondered how Callow would have reacted to his escape. With luck, the governor wouldn't bother sending out a search party, with Ben being so close to release, but Ben wouldn't be trusting to luck and would be mindful of being pursued. If they did come and capture him, then it was unlikely that he would ever see his mother. Callow would kill him and that was a certainty, maybe not straight away but Ben knew that he would have signed his own death warrant, in Callow's eyes, when he had run off.

It was nearly two hours before he made his first stop on the banks of a small stream. The gelding didn't look anything special but had done well so far. As he dismounted he felt the stiffness in his body and he grunted with pain, but he could live with that. While the horse drank from the stream Ben investigated the contents of the food-bag. He broke off a small strip of bread and salted beef and washed it down with the entire contents of the water-bottle; and then he refilled the bottle from the stream.

The next leg of the journey was across open country and, although it would be easier to spot anyone in pursuit, it meant that he had no shelter from the sun. It was a relief when the sun gradually weakened as it slipped into the west and evening approached. He rode on until the darkness made him slow the horse to a walking-pace for fear of its stumbling on uneven ground. The slow, plodding progress soon had him struggling to keep his eyes open and, after nearly falling off for the third time, he pulled it up and dismounted. The moon was now hidden behind some heavy clouds and he found it difficult to find a suitable place to bed down. He eventually settled for a spot close to the trail. He was unsteady on his feet through tiredness as he removed the saddle. He leaned it on a small rock ready to sleep against it. He wasn't sure how safe this spot was but he intended to be on the move at first light, so it didn't matter none that he would be visible from the trail.

Before he drifted into a sleep he heard the scurrying of wildlife but was too tired to be concerned about what might be causing it. Foley had once told him that the difference between animals and people was that God's wild creatures wouldn't bother you if you didn't bother them. He hoped that Foley was right and that it particularly applied to wolves and snakes but he didn't feel confident enough in his friend's theory to remove his boots, even though his feet were aching.

By the time the morning sun awakened him he had enjoyed the first uninterrupted sleep in a long, long time. Usually he was disturbed by the coughing, spitting, screaming and cursing from nearby cells. He stretched to remove his stiffness. It was good to be free, but for how long? And how could he help his brother with each day bringing him closer to the hanging rope?

# 2

By midday as he made his way down a mountain trail he saw the welcome sight of the Tecruna River winding below. This lifted his spirits. He had either made much better progress than he had expected or the map was even less accurate than he suspected it was. So far things had gone well and he remained hopeful that he would make it to Arberstown in time to help his brother or at least comfort his mother. He would cross the river if he could and so reduce the risk of any pursuers trailing him, unless they planned to head direct to Arberstown and catch him there.

When he eventually reached the bottom of the trail he led the gelding close to a shallow inlet of the river to allow it to drink. It had taken him longer to reach the banks of the river than he had expected but he couldn't have risked his mount slipping on the sloping trail. The animal was a hero in his eyes, and when all this was over he would make sure that it got some special pampering. It would enjoy roaming free in the lush grass in the field opposite the Gleason family home.

The sun was high in the sky and it was a relief as he splashed his face and body with the cold water, bringing back memories of his boyhood days in Arberstown when he went fishing with his father. He wondered if he would ever enjoy such carefree days again or would they only be in his dreams? So much would depend on what happened during the next few days. He knew that he never really had a choice other than to try and save his brother's life. But how?

He had just placed his foot in the stirrup when he heard the frantic cry for help. A young boy, about thirteen, was running towards him along the riverbank.

'Please come quick. My brother's drowning.' The boy repeated his plea for the third time and then turned and ran back. Ben gave chase, assuming that the boy had been fishing. By the time Ben caught up with him, he was pointing out towards a spot in the river.

'He slipped off those rocks out there and just went down,' the boy sobbed. 'Please don't let him die.'

Ben had only ever swum in a lake before. This was a fast-flowing river and the boy in trouble could have drifted downstream, but he would have to try and do something. The boy was still screaming at him as Ben pulled off his boots and rushed into the river. The current was far stronger than he had anticipated. He was immediately taken away from the target and within seconds he was no longer thinking in terms of saving the boy but of how he could survive himself. He was soon fifty yards downstream, going wherever the river drew him, with no hope of changing direction. He didn't see the rock that he was thrown against, leaving him dazed but miraculously he was directed into a shallow calm inlet. He shook the drowsiness from his head as he struggled to stand up, his thoughts again turning to the boy in trouble as he waded to the bank and then stumbled along it back to the point where he had entered the water.

He was certain that he hadn't blacked out so he couldn't have been away from the spot for more than a few minutes, but there was no sign of the boy who had called for his help. He looked anxiously towards the rocks, hoping that the boy hadn't followed him into the water in a desperate attempt to save his brother. Then he noticed that his hat was near the spot where he'd left it, but his boots had gone.

He knew he had been duped. He hurried back towards where he had left the gelding just in time to see it being ridden off by a man. The boy who had screamed for help was clinging on to the man with one hand and clutching Ben's boots with the other. Ben ran after them, but stopped as the boy turned and mocked him by waving the boots in the air.

Ben sank to his knees, realizing what a desperate situation he was in. All the excitement of being free and the hope of being able to help his brother had drained away. Seven years in prison should have made him wise to trickery but the boy had made a fool of him. Without a horse and boots, what chance did he have of making it to Arberstown in time to help save Lyle?

He had been a damned fool and there was no denying that but the depression left him as quickly as it had descended on him and he was soon on his feet and walking along the river in the direction of Arberstown. If bad fortune could come his way as it just had then perhaps some good would as well.

The ground near the riverbank was rough in places but the soles of his feet were hardened by the long periods in prison when he was not allowed to wear boots. He felt the sun burning into his back and he was grateful that they hadn't stolen his hat which at least offered his head protection.

He had travelled no more than a mile before he was feeling pain from his knee joints, but at least he had no after-effects from the bump his head had taken on the rocks when he was being swept away. He was thinking about taking a rest when he smelt smoke. His stride quickened as he headed towards the source of the smoke. Almost immediately, he heard the crackle of a fire, then the snorting of a horse, then a rifle being cocked.

'Stop right there or I'll shoot some of those spindly toes off,' shouted the old woman who was pointing a rifle at him.

He stopped in his tracks.

'Hold on, ma'am, I don't mean you any harm.' He was anxious to reassure her that he posed no threat.

The woman's hair was whiter than

spring snow. She was scarcely five feet tall and the wizened face was darkly tanned. Her teeth were clamped on the stem of a pipe. He wondered if she was an Indian because he had never seen a woman smoke a pipe before.

'You won't be doing me no harm, boy. This isn't a stick that I have here and you won't be the first man that I've plugged. I don't need no excuse to kill a man, not after the way they've treated me. Taken what they wanted and then cast me aside. Well, I ain't a slave to no man any more.' She paused and looked down at Ben's feet. 'How come you lost your boots, boy? Most likely fornicating with some man's wife and he caught you at it. Just as well you had your pants on.'

At another time this loopy old woman might have been amusing, but he needed to keep moving and hope for better luck downriver.

'Some low-life and his son stole my horse and boots back there,' he said.

The woman giggled. 'I thought as

much. That was my cousin Bogie and his son Ratty. You're dumber than you look, boy, and that's a fact. How the hell could anyone swim out to those rocks? I could tell you where they live. That's if you want to go and get your things back.'

'I might just kill them if I found them,' he said.

'I don't much like my cousin but there ain't no point in me telling you because he lives the other side of the mountain, and your feet wouldn't make it. Even if you did, then his wild dogs would eat you before you got within smelling distance of him, and that would be some distance away. Bogie gives off a smell stronger than a fish that's been dead for a week.'

'I got to be getting on, lady, so I'll be on my way.'

He sensed some of the hostility had left her.

'So you don't want any of this grub that's just about ready? Never let it be said that Sarah Thomas didn't share her food with all God's creatures.'

Before he could reply she had ordered him to sit down and cross his legs. He was thinking that perhaps she was going to torment him but she was soon pushing a rather dirty plate containing a couple of sizzling fish towards him.

They ate in silence except for when she was spitting out the bones. She carried on smoking her pipe in between eating. Ben was in a desperate plight but he wasn't planning on stealing old Sarah's horse, not that it was an option with her still pointing the gun at him as she ate.

She poured coffee from a kettle into tin cups.

She watched Ben screw his face up as he sipped it. He had been used to watery coffee in prison but this was no ordinary coffee he had been served. It might have been the cause of Sarah's dark-yellow teeth but the extra strong baccy that she smoked had probably helped as well.

'You don't like my coffee then, young fella?' Sarah cackled. Ben decided not to answer her because he would have had to offend her or tell a lie.

With his belly full, Ben stood up, ready to restart his journey but not before he had thanked Sarah again.

'You'd better take those old boots tied to the saddle,' she said, gesturing with a gnarled finger. 'They should fit 'cos I reckon you're about the same size as the fella I took them off last year. I don't know what he died of because the buzzards had been to work by the time I came across him.'

The boots were a perfect fit. Ben noticed quite a few holes had been pecked in them by the buzzards.

'Where're you heading for, son?' Sarah asked, her attitude much friendlier now that she'd had time to weigh him up.

He said, 'Arberstown.'

She scratched the feathery whiskers on her chin.

'I don't know where Arberstown is

but if it's more than a dozen miles downriver then you'd be better off leaving the river trail about a mile from here and then taking the mountain route. It looks a bit daunting but you'll make it now that you have those boots. You'd better take one of those water-bottles because it's going to be hotter than this fire later on.'

When Ben waved goodbye to the strange old lady she gave him a toothy smile. Sarah Thomas might be as hard as they come but, for sure, she also had a soft spot.

As he started the slow climb up the mountain trail he had a fresh determination that he would get to Arberstown in time, no matter what. He resisted the temptation to look back and by the time he stopped to drink from the canteen the river was far below him. He managed a smile when he thought of Sarah down there puffing on her pipe and he wondered how many men she'd terrified. In some strange way she had given him inspiration. She was one gutsy lady. The sun was high in the sky when he reached the top of the mountain and was able to see how the river trail would have taken him way to the east, before swinging back in the direction of Arberstown. The other encouraging thing was that the descent trail back towards the river looked gentler than the one that he had just climbed. After he had seen a couple of snakes slide behind the rocks, he snapped a branch from a small tree. He doubted that it provided much protection, but it made him feel better.

By the time he rejoined the river trail the heat was far more intense and, without the cooling effect of the mountains, he was forced to rest in the shade at regular intervals.

# 3

It was barely light when Callow nudged his sorrel out of the prison gate. It was the day after Gleason had betrayed his trust and made a fool of him by escaping. Nobody made a fool of Lucas Callow and got away with it. If that damned governor had listened to him and allowed him to give chase straight away the killer would be back where he belonged by now. He had always bragged about never having lost a prisoner and some of the guards had made him suffer for his past boasting. During his twenty years as a guard he had been responsible for three deaths but had managed to escape any charges being brought against him. Two prisoners had been half-blinded and another brain-damaged as the result of Callow's boot, but he had always claimed self-defence.

Callow knew exactly where Gleason was heading, thanks to the map that had been supplied by one of the prisoners. Foley had lost most of his teeth and received a broken cheekbone and nose for trying to be loyal to his friend Gleason, but Callow got the information he needed. There was a chance that Gleason might suffer during his futile journey but it would be tame compared to what Callow had in mind for him.

Callow had hated Ben Gleason even before he had been humiliated by him, and had always figured that Gleason should have hanged for the murder he had committed. There was no excuse for taking the law into his own hands just because his old man had lost a fight in a bar-room brawl. It was probably because of the Gleasons' wealthy connections that he'd got off so lightly. It was the old story of one rule for the rich, and another for the poor. Well, Callow had made certain that Ben Gleason hadn't received any special treatment while he was in prison. Over the years Callow had intercepted most of the parcels that had been sent to the rich boy. Why should Gleason have had it easier than the other men just because his mother was loaded?

Callow did have a certain respect for Gleason because he had to admit that he was one tough cookie and perhaps it wasn't so surprising that he would escape to help his brother. He would have known that the odds were stacked against him but that hadn't stopped him trying. Callow was certain that two of Gleason's fellow-prisoners would be wishing that he would perish on the journey. They were the friends of Tony Makin, the man Gleason had killed. The two men had given Gleason a severe beating when he had first arrived in prison and hacked off the trigger finger of his right hand.

The bulging saddles tied to the sorrel's back would ensure that Callow wouldn't run short of food. He had decided that he would have himself a little vacation, mosey around a bit and perhaps stay a while in Arberstown if he was close enough to the town by the time he'd caught up with Gleason. He hadn't had a woman for quite a while, apart from the odd quickie with some of the prison-officer's wives. He figured he was due a few long nights of pleasure. If Gleason was still alive after he had worked him over he could leave him in the custody of the local marshal while he enjoyed himself. He might even pay the lovely Ma Gleason a visit and tell her not to worry about her son because he would make sure that he was well looked after. She might even be grateful to him if she hadn't had a man in all the years since her husband got himself killed. Old Gleason sounded a bit of a weakling and perhaps the rich woman might appreciate a bit of rough like him, they usually did.

Callow roared with laughter at the prospect. One thing he was certain of: Gleason would pay dearly for blemishing his record and embarrassing him.

Not only would Callow make sure that Gleason's life would be hell when they got back to prison, but he would arrange for Gleason to have an 'accident' before his sentence was over. Killers like Gleason shouldn't be allowed to roam free just because some do-gooder of a judge thought he was provoked and too young. Or maybe the judge had taken a bribe. Life had become dull for Callow but now he had a purpose and he was going to make the most of it. When he got back he would make sure that he regained the respect of those who had mocked him.

# 4

Ben hoped that he could remember sufficient details from the map supplied by Crowe which was in the saddlebag of the stolen gelding. He had left the river trail about three miles back although he still got an occasional glimpse of it. He estimated that he had covered almost twenty miles on foot and was now within a day's ride from Arberstown. But, without a horse, he would never arrive by the time his brother had the noose placed around his neck. He'd hoped that by now he would see some familiar landmark or better still a signpost, but he had only been this side of the town a couple of times as a boy, so he wasn't expecting to recognize much. He would rest soon, then bed down for the night at his next stop, but his plan was interrupted by the snorting of a horse behind him.

He stopped and turned around slowly, wondering if it was somebody trailing him. There would be no point trying to run because apart from being too weary he wouldn't get very far against a man on a horse. He should have travelled off-trail to reduce the risk. But he heaved a sigh of relief when he saw the rider. The man certainly wasn't a pursuer from the prison and he was too old to be any kind of lawman.

'Evenin', boy, you're in a strange place to be without a horse.'

Ben was relieved by the friendliness of the man.

'My old nag went lame a couple of miles back and I had to leave him,' Ben lied. 'I was hoping to find some work ahead and maybe buy another animal.'

'Well, there ain't much work between here and Arberstown, but I guess you're heading in my direction so why don't you hitch a ride with me and we can have a chinwag? By the way I'm Silas Deacon. Who might you be?'

Ben had introduced himself as Ben Maple, Maple being his mother's maiden name. There was no point in advertising his true identity.

He wasn't sure the old horse would manage two up but he was desperate to make progress. There was something about Deacon that caused him to trust him even though the years in prison had taught him to be wary of people. It was also good to meet someone who might be described as normal after his earlier experiences but he was still grateful to old Sarah. He'd seen Deacon looking at his clothes and Ben hoped that the old man wasn't the inquisitive sort and would start prying. Sometimes it was easier to tell the truth but he was going to have to lie some if he was to get through the next few days.

Deacon had a smell that reminded Ben of Christmas in prison. That was when the prisoners were given a ration of whiskey, but not much else that could have been described as a treat.

Ben told Deacon that he was heading for Arberstown because he'd heard that there was plenty of work there.

'You'll have a few more blisters by the time you get there. It must be close on forty miles away. Most folks call it Carlisle Town these days rather than Arberstown on account that Kelvin Carlisle owns most of the town and the surrounding land. I don't know what your plans are there but if it's work you're after then you'll finish up working for him one way or the other.'

Ben knew that his torn boots and general appearance must have made Deacon realize that he was lying about losing his horse just a couple of miles away. Ben lied again when he spoke of his plans to join up with a cattle drive near Harpers Post which was about another twenty miles north of Arberstown. Ben hoped that Harpers Post was still a cattle-town, otherwise Deacon might be puzzled by his ignorance.

'There ain't much demand for cattle-men who don't have a horse, fella.'

Silas Deacon's bony little frame rocked with laughter which set off a bout of coughing. It was some time before he was able to speak again.

'I don't like Arberstown much on account of Carlisle and it's a bit too far away for my liking, so I tend to go to a staging post store which is much closer. I do a bit of trading in Arberstown when I have to. As I said, Carlisle owns the town and sets the prices on practically everything. In fact the only place that he doesn't own and control is Connor's undertakers. Mind you, the last time I was in Arberstown, which must have been about four months ago, I did have myself a bit of good fortune. You'll see what I mean when we reach my little palace.'

The mention of the Connors saddened Ben, reviving memories of Mary Jane Connor. They had been sweethearts, nothing serious, with them being so young at the time, but it would have developed but for Ben's untimely departure. Mary Jane had never written to him in prison and his mother had never mentioned her, so he guessed that she and her family were ashamed of what he had done. The family were churchgoing folks and William Connor was a serious sort of man who would have strong views as to whom his daughter should marry. Ben had vague memories of the Carlisles, who owned the neighbouring property, and recalled that his father had won some legal dispute with Kelvin Carlisle over a boundary line. The two families never socialized with each other but Ben remembered that they had a son who was sent East for his schooling. The Carlisle son was supposed to be about the same age as Ben but he had never met him, only seen him from a distance.

By the time they arrived at the shabby-looking cabin, Deacon had just about revealed his life story. Ben guessed that his rescuer didn't get much chance to talk to folks and was making the most of it. He had settled in the area over two years ago after staking a gold-claim, but he had never struck rich and had turned to distilling whiskey. He planned to move closer to a town one day, but he would miss the beauty of the mountain range that he could see from his seat on the cabin porch.

The sight of the grey mare in the corral at Deacon's place had Ben thinking thoughts that he was ashamed of. These were desperate times but he wouldn't want to abuse Deacon's hospitality or face a hanging for being a horse-thief, but he might have to.

The young woman who came running from the cabin would have taken away the breath of any man, let alone one who hadn't seen any woman for nigh on seven years, except for the occasional glimpse of a visitor to the prison. Some of the guards had family living nearby but they were kept well away. Any thoughts that she was Deacon's daughter or even grand-daughter disappeared when she gave

Deacon a lingering kiss on the lips.

'I've meezed you, so mucho,' she said when at last she broke away.

'And I've missed you, Mora honey,' replied Deacon but without sounding very convincing.

Ben had often fantasized about some of the girls who worked in the saloon in Arberstown but none of them compared to Mora. The black hair hung over her bare shoulders and partly covered the ample breasts that strained against the white cotton blouse. The dark-brown eyes were filled with life as she looked Ben up and down. When Deacon introduced them, she offered Ben a deeply tanned hand. Ben felt embarrassed as he realized that he was standing gape-eyed at her beauty. It seemed incredible that the craggy old Deacon had introduced her as 'his woman'. It wasn't exactly beauty and the beast but Deacon was a good sixty-five years old and Mora no more than eighteen.

'Ain't she a beauty?' Deacon asked in

a way that a man might refer to his horse.

'She's very pretty,' Ben replied awkwardly, knowing that 'very pretty' hardly seemed adequate. There were more appropriate ways of describing her, and a goddess would have been one of them. Mary Jane Connor had been pretty but in a different way from this woman.

'She's more than just pretty, son. I can tell you that she can keep a man warm on the coldest night of the winter. If you know what I mean.'

Ben gave a half-smile. He didn't have much experience of women himself except the tales that he'd heard the men in prison tell about what they had done with saloon girls. He remembered Foley advising him never to marry a woman because she looked pretty in her churchgoing clothes. Always marry the girl who stirs you just by being near her. It doesn't matter if she's ugly as long as she makes you want her and she wants you, under the sheets. Foley's philosophy was that you could always tell which husbands had wives who were cold in bed, even on a hot summer's night. They were the miserable and tetchy ones. Foley believed that it was best to marry for lust and passion, never for money — and never if your mother liked the woman.

By the time Ben had finished his meal he knew that Deacon had landed himself more than just one of the most womanly bodies on earth. Burnt beans would have been welcome but the roasted beef and sweet potatoes melted in his mouth. Mora's flashing eyes hardly left Ben and he felt uneasy, knowing that Deacon was no fool and must have seen what was developing between them. Ben started to suspect that Deacon was actually enjoying seeing the flirting that was taking place and he certainly showed no indication that he objected to it.

While the two men talked, Mora cleared away the dishes, pressing her body against Ben when she leaned over to collect his plate. He felt excited in a way that was new to him. This woman was all that Foley had described and much, much more. She knew that she was bringing him pleasure and she was enjoying it herself as she nestled down by Deacon's feet near the fire, making sure that Ben would be looking down into her cleavage. Deacon washed his meal down with a large amount of home-made whiskey and insisted that Ben sampled some of it, but Mora grabbed the glass from Ben's hand. Deacon explained to Ben that she wanted him to have the special Mexican drink that she had prepared for him, so he duly agreed.

Deacon's stories were amusing, but Ben was thinking that it was time he headed for the barn and some much needed sleep in preparation for an early start in the morning. He had decided to steal the horse. Deacon's speech was still clear even after he had finished off a full bottle of whiskey, but then the stories stopped and he began speaking in Mexican with Mora. Ben couldn't understand, but there was no mistaking that Mora was upset about Deacon's drinking. And in addition, Ben was sure they'd been discussing him. The conversation ended with a volley of words from a fiery Mora — an unmistakable example of Mexican cursing.

Deacon sighed with satisfaction.

'I do love a woman with a bit of fire. I could never abide one that fetched and carried and never said boo to a goose. Mind you, there's got to be a limit. My third wife stabbed me whilst I was asleep and would have killed me had the knife not got stuck in my money belt. Then my sixth wife shot me down below and if she'd been a better shot I'd either be dead or speak like a choirboy now.'

'You've been married six times?' asked an astonished Ben.

'Nope, I've been married seven if you count the last one, Dolly. She was more she-devil than a woman but she sure was hot in the sack, almost as good as Mora here.'

Ben's scant knowledge of female anatomy improved when Mora stripped off her blouse, bathed herself from a bowl of water and then turned around to display her magnificent breasts. Ben couldn't tear his eyes away as she thrust them out and traced a finger around the pink circle of one of her nipples.

'Now ain't they a sight for sore eyes? Oh, I forgot to tell you that I won her in a game of poker which is what I meant by my good fortune the last time I was in Arberstown. I don't know who the fella was that lost her but I bet he cries himself to sleep most nights.'

Ben's mouth had gone dry but he managed to tell Deacon that it was time for him to bed down in the barn. This prompted Deacon to flick a hand at Mora and she hurried away towards the tiny bedroom.

'I've got a proposition to put to you, son. Most men would leap at it but I suspect you might not, but just hear me out.'

Ben was taken aback when Deacon

suggested that he slept with Mora. Deacon knew that he had no money or anything worth having so he couldn't intend offering her to Ben in return for some kind of payment. He had heard all about men's exploits with saloon girls and the things that they did for money but this was different.

'I reckon you're just teasing me, Silas. I really must get some sleep. I'm just about done in after all that walking today.' Ben rose from his seat, anxious to get away from the old-timer.

'Sit down, son, and let me explain. This is really important to me, and I mean it when I say that you'll be doing me a big favour.'

Ben reluctantly sat down and wondered what would come next. His parents had been ordinary, regular churchgoing folks and he had no experience of the sort of things that Deacon was proposing. Mora was like an angel, but what was being suggested didn't seem right and proper, especially when he had important matters to attend to, like saving his brother's life.

'Don't look so pained, young fella. I know my suggestion's unusual but it would really help me. I ain't a young man any more as you can plainly see and I'm just not able to provide the needs of a woman like Mora. I was told by a doc who passed this way last week that my condition might pass but the truth is the sap just doesn't rise any more. Giving up whiskey would maybe help, but I don't figure I could do that.'

Ben could see that Deacon was serious and what he said sort of made sense but it still didn't seem proper.

'The fact is Mora will leave me soon if she doesn't get some attention, if you get my drift.'

'But what will she think about this?' asked Ben, beginning to show some interest but still hoping that he could get himself out of this odd situation. 'She seems very fond of you despite the age difference.'

'You know that she's sweet on you, son, and I didn't have to persuade her none when I mentioned it to her. She's a horny little thing and I'd bet you my last bottle of whiskey that she's lying there now, waiting for her needs to be satisfied. So you won't be turning just me down, you'll be turning her down, as well, and if you do I wouldn't expect to get any breakfast in the morning.'

Ben could hardly imagine what it would be like just lying next to her, let alone anything else that might happen. The mere scent of her would be enough to send some men wild and here he was needing to be talked into sleeping with her. He was beginning to think that if he turned down what was being offered he might regret it for the rest of his life.

Deacon was feeling tired and sensed that Ben was weakening. He decided that it was time to close the deal.

'I suspect that you'd like to get to Arberstown in a hurry, son, and if you do as I ask I'll lend you the grey mare tomorrow and trust that you'll bring it back when you've sorted out yourself a horse of your own. Oh, and by the way, if you were thinking of stealing her in the night I warn you that I'm a very light sleeper and I don't take kindly to thievin'. In my book stealing a man's horse is worse than stealing his wife and one of the few things that I would shoot a man in the back for. There might be something wrong with my pleasure bits down below but there ain't nothing wrong with my hearing or eyesight.'

Ben was still in a state of confusion when he eventually agreed to go along with the bizarre suggestion. He could have easily overpowered Deacon now and ridden off, but not without hurting him and that was something he wasn't prepared to do.

'Good, now you go in there and I'll be off to the barn,' Deacon said. 'I'll see you in the mornin' and don't start feeling guilty. You'll be riding out of here tomorrow and no one will have been harmed. If you carry out your side of the bargain, I expect to hear Mora singing at breakfast.'

Ben slowly rose from his chair and

walked towards the room where the waiting Mora was, half-expecting to hear Deacon roar with laughter and tell him that he had only been kidding. He swung around when he heard the main door of the cabin slam shut, confirming that Deacon was on his way to the barn and leaving him free to spend the night in a way that he could never have imagined.

Mora had the top half of her body covered as she lay on the bed. For a moment Ben felt foolish and awkward. A man who had survived amongst criminals and hardcases shouldn't be intimidated by an eighteen-year-old girl. It should have been the other way around. He should have been about to help her overcome her innocence, not that she had any. Old Deacon surely wasn't the only man that she'd had.

'Are you sure that you want this to happen?' asked Ben, his speech was thick and his mouth dry, forgetting that Mora probably didn't understand him. Whether she understood him or not she made her feelings clear when she peeled back the sheet and revealed the full nakedness of her body.

'Jesus,' he gasped as he stared down at her beauty. Mora's face was flushed with excitement as she got off the bed and started to unbutton Ben's shirt. She rubbed the hard muscles on his chest and murmured with satisfaction.

The night was filled with a mixture of pleasure and guilt as his hunger for Mora was matched by her desire for him. Before she had finally drifted into sleep Ben had stopped her crying by promising that he would take her with him when he left in the morning.

# 5

Kelvin Carlisle had gone to considerable trouble to secure his ambitions for his son, Errol and now everything was being threatened by someone whose only asset was a pretty face. Most women would have broken off their engagement if they discovered that their fiancé had spent the night with the whores of the Drinking Well saloon, but not little Missy Connor. Kelvin Carlisle had arranged for one of the girls to taunt her about what she could expect on her wedding night but it had made no difference. The stupid girl had cried for awhile but quickly forgave Errol when he blamed it on the drink. So having done his best to split them up, Carlisle had to go through the motions of giving them his blessing.

He planned to purchase the nearby Gleason ranch and give it to his son as a wedding present but he was determined to have the property for another reason. The Gleason property was flanked by land owned by Carlisle and obtaining it would make Carlisle the sole owner of the largest single piece of land in the whole of the state. He had been so confident of completing the purchase that he had told some of his friends back East that the deal was done. But he had miscalculated the stubbornness of Evelyn Gleason. She had refused to sell. Carlisle didn't doubt that the property would become his eventually but he was impatient.

Then just over a month ago some news came his way that gave him some fresh hope for his son's future. Perhaps he wouldn't be having Mary Jane Connor for a daughter-in-law after all. Now while he waited for his ranch manager and enforcer, Sol Ackroyd, to arrive he was hoping that this dreadful business would soon be at an end.

Kelvin Carlisle had become the richest man in the state by being ruthless and having a flair for business was how an Eastern newspaper described his success but it was far from the truth. He had been motivated by his desire to make amends for the failure of his father who had committed suicide after he was made bankrupt. Some years later Carlisle had inherited a large sum of money from his grandfather but had wasted much of it on failed businesses back East. When he came West he started out with a modest cattle business even though he had no experience or interest in raising cattle. It was the early 1870s when he started to specialize in providing loans to those whom the bank considered a risk. Carlisle had obtained money from the banks by lying about his own assets and forging documents that he had presented as security.

It wasn't the first time that he had used deception and fraud to mask his failures. Kelvin Carlisle had been heading for bankruptcy and a jail sentence when he was saved by the horrific droughts between 1873 and

1874. The cruel act of nature had devastated cattle businesses both large and small but it resulted in Carlisle acquiring large numbers of the failed businesses because the owners were unable to pay back the loans to him. When the market recovered a few years later it made Carlisle a very, very rich man.

He had always been disappointed in his son but was hopeful that with a bit of maturity he would be capable of great things. With his father's wealth and influence there was no reason why he shouldn't be state governor one day. If that happened he would need a wife who would be able to socialize and help her husband's career. Mary Jane Connor wasn't his idea of a governor's wife, not by a long chalk. She would be an embarrassment just as Errol's mother, Heather, would have been to him but he had been spared that problem. Although Errol was a frequent visitor to his mother's grave on the Carlisle estate his father had never been seen there and it disgusted a few of the old timers who had attended her burial the day after Errol was born.

Sol Ackroyd had been dreading his meeting with Carlisle and when he was ushered into Carlisle's drawing room and saw the grim look on Carlisle's face it didn't make him feel any better. Carlisle's well groomed silver hair and thin, almost pinched features gave him the appearance of a city banker rather than a ruthless cattle baron. The heavy lines on the face and the half closed eye, the result of a mild stroke, were testimony that power and wealth had not brought him happiness.

Carlisle flicked his hand as a signal for Ackroyd to sit down. There was no warmth or appreciation towards the man who had worked for him for many years.

'It's been a month since we discussed Ben Gleason so I expect to hear some good news on that front,' Carlisle announced.

Ackroyd had no news at all but he

wasn't about to admit that to Carlisle. Why should he risk a tongue-lashing from the old devil when Gleason might show up at any time?

'My contacts have assured me that he's heading this way and should be in town any day soon.'

'And you are certain that this Ben Gleason and Mary Jane Connor were really close before he was sent to prison?' said Carlisle in between puffs on the large cigar.

'As I explained last time, Mr Carlisle, the folks I spoke to reckoned they were sweethearts ever since they were kids and would definitely have married but for him killing a man.'

'I've been thinking about this idea of yours, Ackroyd, and I can't see the Connor girl giving Errol up for a man whom she has never even visited all the time he's been in jail.'

'I think that was because William Connor forbade her from having anything to do with Gleason after he'd been sentenced,' Ackroyd explained.

'That damned undertaker. First he refuses to sell his business to me and now he's about to lumber me with his scatty daughter. So this contact of yours has arranged for Gleason to escape from prison or did you manage to bribe someone?'

As Ackroyd started to answer, Carlisle interrupted him.

'On second thoughts I don't want to know the details. Just make sure that he gets here soon and picks up where he left off with Mary Jane Connor.'

Carlisle picked up some papers from his desk and started reading them. This was Ackroyd's cue to leave.

'Oh, there is one other thing,' Carlisle called out as Ackroyd reached the door. 'I'm a bit concerned about Miss Connor riding out here alone. I would hate my son's fiancée to have some lusty cowhand force himself upon her in some lonely spot.'

Ackroyd left the house feeling that he had handled things well. Now he would have to hope that the money he had spent to bring Ben Gleason back to Arberstown would not have been wasted. Ackroyd had considered bribery as the method of getting an early release for Gleason but had dropped the idea because it was too risky. He would find out soon enough if his idea had worked and if not there was always Carlisle's suggestion about Mary Jane Connor. He wouldn't need to find anyone for that task. He had always fancied her, ever since her hips had filled out and her breasts were now more than a good handful. No, that one would be what you might call a labour of pleasure. Errol Carlisle wouldn't want the shame of marrying soiled goods, especially if she ended up with a swollen belly. He would try getting Gleason home first, but he didn't plan to wait too long before turning his attention to the ripened Mary Jane Connor. Nature hadn't been kind to Ackroyd. The pug nose and almost permanent sneer on his face gave the impression that he was a simpleton.

He was a powerfully built man and many of Carlisle's hired hands had suffered after misjudging him.

# 6

Mora was still sleeping when Ben crept from the bed and gazed down at her, knowing that he would never see a woman more beautiful than her. He had been awake for the past hour, his head spinning with thoughts of his brother, his mother, young sister and Mora. Perhaps if he ever got to return with the 'borrowed' horse he might get to see her again.

By the time Ben had washed in the horse trough, Deacon had brought out the fully saddled mare.

'There's some grub in the saddlebag, son, so you can get on your way. Maybe it'd be best if you kept the mare and didn't come by here again. If you want to pay me you can always leave something with Charlie the barman at Sharkey's saloon.'

Ben was glad he would be able to

leave without seeing Mora again because he knew that it would have been difficult. They had talked about lots of things last night after he had discovered that she could speak more English than Deacon believed she could. Now in the cold light of day everything seemed different, and he was wishing that he hadn't said certain things to her.

Deacon had told him to follow the river for about five miles and cross at Bolan's Creek. If he rode hard then he should be in Arberstown before dark. Ben thanked Deacon for his help and promised that he would leave payment for the horse and saddle at the saloon. Ben wondered if Deacon was now regretting allowing him and Mora their night of pleasure and thinking that it wasn't such a good idea after all.

The mare produced a good turn of speed and Ben's troubles were forgotten for the moment as he enjoyed the pleasure of riding again. The mare was no match for the black stallion that his father had given him for his sixteenth birthday, but it still felt good.

The closer he got to Arberstown the more beautiful was the scenery. It helped to take his mind off things, but not for long. It wasn't surprising that his father had chosen to live out West even though he wasn't a rugged man. The Gleason family had made their fortune manufacturing saddles and leather goods and when his father had arranged to have the magnificent farmhouse built on the vast estate it was mainly for his family's future. The plan was that one day his sons would farm the land or raise cattle and he would look after the business side of things. On the night he was murdered he had made a rare visit to the saloon in Arberstown to have a beer. A chance meeting with a drunken thug had ended with him dying on the bar-room floor.

Ben had gone to town with his father and had been collecting some stores for his mother when someone had come running to tell him what had happened.

The bearer of the news had named the thug as Tony Makin, a man who was known as a local troublemaker.

When Ben had entered the saloon Doc Sloane was tending his father who was laid out on a long table. The shake of the doctor's head and the grimness of his expression confirmed Ben's fears. He had paused only momentarily to touch his pa before finding Makin.

During his years in prison Ben had relived the taunts that Makin had made after Ben had threatened to kill him. Makin had still been mocking Ben as he went for his gun but his smirking changed to shock as the bullet from Ben's gun ripped into his stomach.

Ben had felt no emotion as he walked over to Makin's fallen body and fired another shot into the side of his head.

Before that night Ben had fired no more than a couple of dozen practice shots since he had been given the gun for his eighteenth birthday, just a week earlier. He had begged his parents for weeks before they had eventually given in to his wishes. The gun had cost him his freedom but he harboured no regrets for his actions.

He wondered what changes he would see in Arberstown now that this man Carlisle had exerted his influence. His mother had never mentioned him or his family but Deacon certainly didn't think much of the man. Ben had no real idea of how he was going to help his brother escape but he would need a gun.

Ben had not ridden the old mare too hard, figuring that as long as he made it close enough to Arberstown before nightfall there was a chance he could help his brother. Despite his caution, everything was thrown into jeopardy after the third stop of the day. The mare refused to move off after he nudged her with his heels. He decided that perhaps if he walked her for a while she might recover her strength, but further attempts to ride her failed after just a short distance.

He wondered if Deacon had known

that the horse wouldn't make it to Arberstown. Perhaps the old-timer wasn't such a likeable rogue after all.

Ben dismounted and led the animal towards a clump of trees. He tethered her, and then removed the saddle. He would rest the animal for a couple of hours in the hope that she might recover. There was no sign of any injury and it could be just a matter of tiredness or old age.

* * *

Ben had used the saddle as a headrest but fought against sleeping in case it might delay his journey. Being in a sort of half-sleep prevented him from seeing the rider who had dismounted just feet away. By the time his eyes focused on Lucas Callow his pursuer's pistol was on its way to striking him across the side of the face. Ben managed to turn his head just enough to avoid the full impact, then he struggled to his feet. Callow threw his gun to the ground and gestured to Ben to come towards him, confident of getting the better of a man who was weakened by years on meagre prison rations.

'Come on, boy. You might get lucky,' Callow taunted and then laughed.

Ben stood his ground. He was in no hurry to start a fight that he knew he would lose. He had seen the brutality of Callow in action too many times to know that it couldn't be any different.

'Come on, little rich boy. Ain't you got any balls?' Callow teased him and then prodded Ben in the chest.

Ben decided that he might as well get it over with and swung a punch that caught the surprised Callow on the side of his face, causing a split on his cheek that produced a trickle of blood. The blow had hurt Callow and made him stagger but he shrugged it off.

'If that's your best shot, then you're in big trouble, you backshooter. Now let's show you what real fighting's all about.'

The first swinging punch from

Callow missed its mark but the second caught Ben full on the nose. If the punch hadn't broken the nose then the butt that followed certainly did. Ben didn't see any of the punches that followed before Callow held him up while he delivered three butts in succession before letting the limp body drop to the ground.

As Ben drifted in and out of consciousness he was thinking of his night with Mora. Then he realized that he had been tied to his saddle, denying him any real movement of his legs or arms. He made a feeble attempt to free himself but he was too weak. The side of his face and nose ached and judging by the stains on his shirt he had lost plenty of blood.

He could see the blurred figure of Callow who was drinking from a bottle.

'Well that's a pity. I was hoping you were dead. I must be losing my touch.'

Callow's words were slurred. 'I'm just going to finish this bottle and then we'll push on into Arberstown. I'll leave you with the marshal while I have me some fun. You might even get to share a cell with that killer brother of yours. Now wouldn't that be nice. That's if your brother really is going to hang. After you left there was some talk that the fella who told you about your brother had made the whole thing up. I wonder why he would have done that.'

There was a ringing in Ben's ears and he couldn't hear everything that Callow was saying, but he heard enough to understand.

'I've been thinking that if the saloon girls are a juicy bunch, I might stay an extra night. It will give you more time to get over seeing your brother's face go purple and black while dangling from a rope. Of course he'll probably squeal like a pig when they put the noose on. They usually do.'

Ben was relieved when Callow developed a bout of hiccups, giving him some respite, but it wasn't long before the taunts started again.

'I wonder if your ma is still a good-looking woman. I remember her coming to see you once and thinking what a waste it was going to be. A lovely body like that curling up alone every night. I bet she must be begging for it by now unless she's shacked up with some lucky fella. I might just pay her a call and tell her how I was passing through and wanted her to know that I was looking after you. She'll be upset about your brother and a night in the sack with me will be just what the doctor ordered.'

While Callow roared with laughter Ben strained at the ropes that secured him. If he could free himself, he swore he would get the better of his tormentor. The laughter finally stopped but it wasn't long before the silence was broken by Callow's grunting and snoring. Ben eventually gave up trying to free his hands and drifted into a deep sleep, weakened by his efforts and loss of blood.

When he eventually came awake, he

was shivering with cold although the sun was shining. Night had come and gone. At first he had no idea where he was until the pain reminded him of events. He looked over at Callow who was flat on his back. He must have fallen into a drunken sleep, and would be mad, when he awoke, to find he'd missed his night in Arberstown.

Ben closed his eyes to block out the early-morning sun, but heard a sound coming from where Callow lay. Raising his head, Ben saw maybe up to a dozen rats raiding the contents of Callow's saddlebags which lay beside him. Ben's call to Callow didn't arouse him but the rats scurried away. After several louder calls to Callow brought no response, Ben studied the pallor of Callow's face and realized the reason for his silence. Lucas Callow was dead and Ben would join him unless someone came by or he managed to free himself. He remembered his failed efforts of last night and he wasn't feeling any stronger despite a night's rest.

He had an idea that might just work, but it would be risky. He would need the help of the rats which had just returned and were once again nuzzling into the contents of Callow's saddle-bags.

# 7

Evelyn Gleason had spent another night weeping. She could still turn men's heads wherever she went into Arberstown even though she was forty-five-years old but life had been cruel to her. She had been robbed of her husband and soon her younger son would be dead. Not the honourable death of a young soldier but that of a self-confessed killer. His life seemed to have offered so much promise, but now it would end in disgrace.

She had often wondered how different it would have been if her dear husband, Milton, had not gone into town that night. Her son Ben would not be in prison and Lyle would not have changed the way he had. She had made her decision that she wouldn't go to see Lyle in jail, knowing that he would blame her for what had happened, and she couldn't bear that. There had been moments during the night when she had found herself thinking that perhaps she should end her nightmare, but what would become of Clarissa? How would she cope with such tragedy? Then Evelyn reminded herself that Ben would be home soon and things would get better.

But what if Ben had changed under the harshness of prison life? Perhaps he wouldn't even return to Arberstown after what had happened, especially when he heard about Lyle. He would think that the family name would be despised — and then there was Mary Jane. How would he feel when he found out that Mary Jane was going to be married? Evelyn had wanted to tell him but thought that it was best that he should hold on to his dreams for a while longer. She still hoped that perhaps Mary Jane's wedding to Errol Carlisle wouldn't go ahead, because the girl would be making a big mistake. Errol Carlisle might be the son of the richest man in the state but he wasn't the man for Mary Jane.

Over recent months Evelyn hadn't been able to reason with Lyle. He couldn't understand why the family was short of money, claiming that both his father's family and Evelyn's had been wealthy. Evelyn had lied to him in order that he wouldn't waste the money that had been left in trust for all her children and to help renovate the property that had been neglected in recent years. The hired hands had become fed up with Lyle and his drunken rages and they had all left after he had reduced their wages in order to pay for his gambling habit. Some of them had spread the word that working for the Gleasons wasn't a good idea.

Evelyn had longed for the day when the family would be reunited and the property restored to its former glory, which was why she had resisted the pressure from Kelvin Carlisle to sell it to him. Carlisle had shown some interest in her in a clumsy way a few months ago, but she detested the man and disliked his son, who had introduced Lyle to gambling and given him fancy ideas that he couldn't afford.

That evening, Evelyn had gone on to her favourite spot on the porch, sitting in a rocker, so that she could look across the valley at the view that she and Milton had fallen in love with. Before the house was built, they had stood on the hill at this very spot.

She would need to keep busy in order to keep her mind off things. When it was all over she would visit the grave, just the once. Some mothers will always forgive their children but she couldn't find it in her heart to do so. People might think her heartless for not accepting the marshal's offer to allow a normal family funeral because of Lyle being so young. He could have been buried near his father on the hillside that they owned, but she wanted no privileges for her killer son.

The sight of dust rising from the trail had her standing up to get a clearer view. It was rare to have visitors, especially so late in the evening. Her mind raced as she wondered if it could be Ben, released early, perhaps bringing someone whom he had met up with.

'Please God, let it be my Ben,' she muttered to herself.

By the time the riders came close, her eyes were once again filled with tears. 'Clarissa,' she called to her daughter, 'it's your brother!'

# 8

The sight of Arberstown ahead caused a stir of excitement in Ben and some anxiety as he wondered once more whether anyone would recognize him. He could still feel his nose throbbing along with the pain from where the rats had bitten his hands but his idea of smearing the ropes with food had worked. It had been difficult dragging himself and the saddle he was tied over to where the food had spilled on the ground. He hadn't been able to stop the food from getting on to his hands but enough had gone on to the ropes to entice the rats to gnaw into it.

Now he was thinking that the prison authorities might have telegraphed the marshal in Arberstown and given him a description. It had all seemed so clear to him when he had planned his escape, but now he felt that he had been a fool.

It was also likely that he would be suspected of having killed Callow when the guard didn't return to the jail. Ben had wanted to bury Callow but it would have cost him valuable time. Now he wished that he had, but in truth he had more concern for Deacon's old mare, which he had let roam free when he had opted to use Callow's horse.

He had spent the last few miles wondering, not for the first time, if his brother deserved his help. Lyle had been just an innocent boy when he last saw him but the question was what sort of a man had he become?

Main Street looked much the same as he remembered except that a second saloon had been built next to the hotel. His eyes were drawn to the man standing outside the marshal's office wearing a shiny badge. The thickset man wasn't Marshal Carter, who had arrested him, and that at least was good news. The marshal gave him a cursory glance and Ben hoped that Callow's loose-fitting clothes would not attract any special attention. He reckoned that it must be between ten o'clock and noon and the first thing he needed to do was to confirm when his brother was to be hanged, praying that he wasn't too late. He didn't plan on asking the marshal. The one man whom he could ask was Jack Kearney, an old friend of his father. Jack had been a blacksmith and his premises used to be at the other end of town and that was where Ben headed.

The blacksmith's was still there but the sign outside read CARLISLE'S not KEARNEY'S and the man hammering at the hoof of a horse certainly wasn't Jack.

Ben hadn't liked taking Callow's money or stripping him of his clothes to replace his own. The money would certainly come in handy and his first call was to the store, having decided that the marshal wouldn't have been outside his office watching the world go by if a hanging was imminent. Ben intended purchasing a left-handed holster, a pair of Levis and a new shirt. He decided to keep the boots given to him by old Sarah. Perhaps they would bring him luck even though they hadn't helped their previous owner! He remembered Deacon's comments about the price fixing by Carlisle, although Ben wouldn't be able to judge the price of anything, having been out of circulation for so long. Henry Mortimer had served Ben on many occasions but he showed no sign that he had recognized Ben. Ben remembered him as a kind man and he wasn't surprised when the storekeeper gave him a generous allowance on Callow's old holster.

Ben was anxious to leave the store as quickly as possible when he saw young Lily Mortimer appear from behind the counter. He turned away from her before she had the chance to see him properly, fearing that she might show him more attention than her pa had.

Ben entered the barber's shop that was next to the store hoping that this was where he would find out about Lyle. The bald-headed proprietor, who had the sniffles, didn't look familiar, nor did he look very happy. Ben asked for a very light trim of his shaggy black hair but opted to leave his beard as it was. The less he looked like the Ben Gleason who had left town seven years ago, the safer he would feel.

'I heard there was going to be a hanging here today,' Ben said, trying to sound as casual as he could.

'Eight o'clock this morning,' the barber replied and sniffed once again.

Ben felt his heart sink. He was too late! His worst nightmare had come true. He had risked so much and it was all for nothing.

'Or at least it would have been if Lyle Gleason hadn't escaped two nights ago and killed his cell mate, Jeb Doran, whose only crime was being drunk. The way folks feel about Gleason around here, they won't be waiting for a lawful hanging if they catch him. Not after what he did after he escaped. As if killing one man wasn't bad . . . '

The barber shook his head in disgust. Clearly it pained him just to talk about it and he didn't finish his sentence.

Ben hadn't contemplated the possibility of his brother escaping without his help. For a moment he was staggered by the news. What should he do now? He didn't ask any more questions, seeing how the barber felt about Lyle. When the barber had finished Ben took a bath in the tiny room at the back of the shop and then changed into his newly acquired Levis and shirt. Callow's clothes had hung loose on him and he had lost the feeling of self-consciousness when he left the barber's ready to start the journey to the Gleason ranch . . . home!

There would have been a welcoming party arranged by his mother once his official release date had been announced. Now everything had changed.

His mother had only visited him once and it had left her so upset that he had insisted that she never came again. By now, she would have aged, perhaps prematurely after all that had happened. But she was a beautiful woman and a loving one and he promised himself that somehow he would make things easier for her. Money had never been a problem for the family but it was the emotional side that would have hit her hard. All this trouble with Lyle would have added to her distress and it was all so damned unfair.

His sister Clarissa would be about ten and in no time at all the young bucks would come calling on her. Ben would be expected to take the decisions as the man of the house, but he was ready to do that. Makin had deserved to die for murdering his father but Ben had often agonized about how much his taking the law into his own hands had hurt his mother.

He was within a few hundred yards of the trail that led towards the Gleason property when two riders appeared, headed in his direction. He lowered his left hand closer to his gun as a precaution. The riders must have come off the Gleason property and it was possible they were enquiring about his escape, though he thought that unlikely. Why would the prison authorities send men after him when he was so close to release? He reasoned that it would be too soon for anyone to have found Callow's body, and anyway he had died from natural causes. Then he remembered the bruises on Callow's face that he'd caused during their brief fight.

Ben's fears faded when he saw that one of the riders was a woman whom he knew, but the man was a stranger. Ben gave them the briefest nod, making no attempt to hide his face. If Mary Jane Connor recognized him it didn't really matter now. She gave him a faint smile; she looked pale and drawn, but even more beautiful than he remembered. The man riding with her eyed him suspiciously. He was dressed in a city suit with the coat pulled back revealing a double holster. Ben took an instant dislike to him.

Ben resisted the temptation to call after Mary Jane, sensing that his attention would not have been welcome. He was certain that she had recognized him but there had been no indication that she was pleased to see him. The Connors had always been close to his family and they had helped his ma through her bereavement, not just because William Connor was an undertaker but because they were friends. Ben believed that William Connor was also a fair man who would accept him once he had served his sentence, and would not object to Ben renewing his relationship with Mary Jane.

Seeing Mary Jane had made Ben eager to start rebuilding his life. After he had seen his mother he would give himself up to the marshal and hope that his sentence wouldn't be increased by too much because he had escaped. At least he had no need to fear Lucas Callow.

The Gleason sign above the gate at the main entrance to the house brought a lump to his throat. He was home even though it would only be for a short while. Rounding the curved section of trail he saw the house up on the hill and he marvelled just how magnificent it was. During his early days in prison Ben had written to his mother and tried to encourage her to move back East because life would have been easier for her, but she had replied that she would never leave.

As Ben got closer to the house his excitement turned to a sense of unease. There was something wrong. The atmosphere was so strange. It wasn't just the sight of the neglected house with its peeling paintwork and other signs of neglect. There were no animals. His dog Callum might have died but Laddie and Taffy had only been pups when he left and there was no sign of the goats that kept the grass near the house under control. His mother had always been a capable and practical woman and would have kept things in order, especially with Lyle's help. None of this made sense to him as he recalled her last letter in which she seemed so happy. She had told him how pretty and clever Clarissa was and they were all looking forward to the day when he would be released.

Ben dismounted and tried all the doors of the house but they were securely locked. He looked through a gap in the curtains but was unable to get a proper view inside. He was tempted to ride after Mary Jane Connor to find out what had happened to his mother and sister, but opted to have a good look around before returning to Arberstown.

Inspection of the various outbuildings revealed the same level of neglect as the house. The bunkhouse was open but it was obvious that it had not been occupied recently. It was going to be some time before he could live out the dreams that had enabled him to survive in prison.

On the ride back to town he tried to stay positive. There might be an explanation and perhaps things were not as bad as he feared. Perhaps his mother had gone back East after the recent upset with Lyle. Whatever the reason was he felt sure that Mary Jane would have the answer.

When Ben passed near the marshal's office the lawman was talking to the man who had been with Mary Jane. Ben sensed that the men were talking about him and he heeled his mount on a little faster when he saw Mary Jane outside the main store. She was holding the hand of a young girl and he had a sudden sinking feeling that maybe Mary Jane might be married. But the girl was too old to have been Mary Jane's.

Ned Brewster liked Errol Carlisle even less than he did his father but he couldn't ignore what he had just told him. Brewster had been marshal of Arberstown for almost two years and he was thinking that at the age of fifty-six perhaps it was time to be handing in his badge. He had seen a number of killings since his time in office, even though Arberstown was a quieter town than most. But the incident two nights ago had deeply troubled Brewster. It wasn't just a tragedy, it was a disgrace as far as he was concerned. Jeb Duran had been killed whilst he was in custody, just for the night because he had been a nuisance after getting drunk.

A lot of unusual things had occurred in recent weeks and feelings had been running high. Brewster had expected to be blamed for not staying overnight at his office and the criticism was probably justified, even though he had hardly slept for the previous three nights and was still recovering from a recent gunshot wound. Perhaps he should have kept his deputy on duty instead of letting him go home to be with his wife who was about to give birth. Brewster figured that once word of the killing got to Kelvin Carlisle, then any thoughts about retiring might be taken out of his hands because Carlisle would get him sacked.

Brewster had no doubt that Kelvin Carlisle considered himself above the law and would prefer to have his own man as marshal, but surprisingly most of the town council had opted to keep Brewster in office. Carlisle hadn't pushed too hard to replace Brewster so far, but he might seize the opportunity now unless the marshal managed to redeem himself. The information that Errol had just passed on might possibly get Brewster out of trouble but he was puzzled as to why Errol had been so forthcoming.

Ben dismounted and tied his horse to the hitch rail close to where Mary Jane was engaged in a conversation with the girl. He smiled at Mary Jane when she looked in his direction but she didn't return the smile and seemed nervous as she looked away and towards the marshal's office.

'Mary Jane, it's me, Ben,' he called out.

He was disappointed that she showed no signs of surprise or excitement as she replied.

'Yes, I know. I saw you near your house.'

He felt a sudden sense of guilt about his time with Mora.

The pretty blond-haired little angel with Mary Jane didn't need any introduction. He could see his mother's looks in the shy, frightened face.

'Clarissa, this is your brother, Ben.'

Ben was startled when the girl backed away from him, burying her face into Mary Jane's side like a terrified baby.

'I'm sorry. She's still frightened after . . . ' Mary Jane's voice tailed off.

'Mary Jane, do you know where my mother is?' Ben asked fearing that Mary Jane was hiding something from him as he saw the tears well in her eyes. Suddenly she turned and hurried away clasping Clarissa's hand.

Ben was left feeling anxious and puzzled but his thoughts were interrupted by the loud voice behind him.

'Mister, are you Ben Gleason?'

Ben turned to see that the question

had been asked by the marshal. He guessed Mary Jane's riding companion, who was standing next to the marshal, must have told the lawman who he was.

'Yes, I am. I was going to see you later and give myself up. I guess you know that I escaped from the Cragoma Plains prison.'

The marshal drew his pistol and pointed it at Ben.

'I didn't, but I'm arresting you for helping your brother escape from a hanging, and for killing Jeb Doran and your own mother. Now undo that belt real slow and drop it on the ground!'

Ben felt that he was in the middle of a nightmare and his instinct was to draw his gun and take his chances. Something crazy was happening here and he was about to become a victim of it. He had been stunned by the news of his mother. Surely, it had to be a mistake. She couldn't be dead. Not now after he was so close to being reunited with her and ready to make life sweeter for her.

'Now you're my witness, Errol,' said the marshal, keeping his eyes fixed on Ben. 'I told this son of a bitch he was under arrest and if I have to shoot him in the next few seconds it's of his own making. Now drop that belt, Gleason, or you can die here and save the town a hanging.'

Ben was within a whisker of going for his gun but decided that wasn't the answer to the mess he was in, but he would have liked to wipe the smirk off Errol's face.

He fumbled to undo the belt with his deformed right hand which had the trigger finger missing and let the belt hit the dirt in front of him.

'Your accusations are crazy, Marshal,' he said. 'I was miles away from here when my brother escaped and I haven't seen my dear mother for years. What I say is true and I swear it on my little sister's life.'

'Save your bleating for the jury and start heading for my office back there.'

The marshal positioned himself behind

Ben and prodded him in the back with his gun. A small group of men had gathered and were eager to know what the marshal was up to with the stranger who was now begrudgingly walking in the direction of the jail.

'What's happening, Marshal?' someone called out.

The marshal wished that Errol Carlisle hadn't answered for him and told the crowd that the stranger was Ben Gleason and that he'd killed his mother.

'Why don't you take the posse out again, Marshal, and bring that swine of a brother back, then we can have a double hanging,' one of the group shouted.

'Why wait? Let's hang this mother-killer now. Someone fetch a rope,' another cried.

Carlisle had just made the marshal's job much harder. The lawman turned his gun away from Ben's back and fired two shots into the air, causing the mob to halt in their tracks.

'There'll be no lynching in this town and I'll drop the first man that tries,' Marshal Brewster yelled. 'Now go about your business and leave this to the law.'

The rebel-rousers had seen Brewster in action. They backed down, deciding to bide their time, for the present at least.

The trio with Ben in the lead reached the jail without further incident and Brewster ordered his deputy, Mickey Ives, to stand guard outside and to discourage any troublemaker who tried to enter the jail. Ives sensed that there was real trouble brewing. Perhaps it was time to try a different job now that he was a father.

Ben was pushed into one of the cells, still finding it hard to take in what was happening to him. He had so many questions to ask but first he needed to know about his mother.

'Your ma died two nights ago, just after your brother escaped, as if you didn't know,' Carlisle told him, answering for the marshal once again.

'I've already explained that I wasn't anywhere near Arberstown then. I only arrived here a couple of hours ago. And why would I or my brother want to kill our own mother? The idea is just so crazy. If I'd done such a horrible thing or had any part in it, would I have come back into Arberstown?'

The marshal sighed and shook his head.

'The reason you killed her is one of the oldest motives in the world, greed and money. Errol's father, Kelvin, wanted to buy your mother out but she refused to sell. So, you and your brother tried to force her, and one of you strangled her. Then you thought that you would show up, act the innocent and then after your mother was buried today you could sell up and share the blood-money with your brother.'

Marshal Brewster had Errol to thank for providing all the pieces about motive. He hadn't believed it himself at first but it certainly fitted together nicely enough to convince a jury.

'I'd better be getting back to Mary Jane, Marshal,' said Carlisle.

'Sure thing,' Brewster acknowledged. 'And thanks for your help with this mess.'

Errol gave Ben a final look of disgust and left the jailhouse, leaving Ben wondering how serious the relationship was between Carlisle and Mary Jane.

'By the way, your sister is being cared for by Mary Jane Connor and her family. Mary Jane is due to marry Errol this year but I'm sure they'll make suitable arrangements for Clarissa.'

When the marshal walked away from the cell Ben lay down on the hard bed and tried to fathom how this nightmare could have happened. He tried convincing himself that the truth must come out, even though it wouldn't help bring his ma back. Then he remembered men in prison who swore to him that they were innocent and he had believed some of them. The one thing that kept nagging him was how his brother could be so different from the one that his mother had described in her letters. Ben had seen with his own eyes that his brother had not helped stop their fine home falling into its present state and he had confessed to killing one man and might have killed another. But surely he couldn't have killed their dear mother! The very thought that his own kin could do such a thing made Ben shudder, but then his anger began to build. The fact was that he knew nothing about his brother, except that he was a self-confessed killer. The marshal was right about one thing, his mother would never have sold their property.

As frustration swirled inside him, Ben stood up and went to the cell door, desperate to know more about his mother's death.

'Marshal, I need to talk to you,' Ben shouted.

'Then don't go barking out orders to me. What is it?' Brewster approached the cell.

'Marshal, how can you be so sure

who killed my mother?'

'Because I have a witness,' Brewster replied without smugness but with conviction.

'You have a witness who saw me and my brother together? It wouldn't happen to be that sly fella, Carlisle?'

'The witness didn't exactly see you together and it wasn't Errol Carlisle. I doubt if even you will challenge her. It was your young sister, Clarissa.'

Ben remembered how she had recoiled from him, clearly frightened, perhaps even terrified. If he had thought that his nightmare couldn't have got any worse, it just had.

'But Clarissa was only three years old when she last saw me before today, and I don't look anything like I did then. How could she possibly identify me?'

The marshal showed slight hesitation.

'Hmm, she didn't actually say that she saw you. On the night your mother was murdered Clarissa was in her room at the big house. She looked out of the window and saw two men approaching the house, just before your mother shouted to her that her brother was coming, but Clarissa decided to stay in her room. She heard a lot of arguing and raised voices but apparently that wasn't uncommon, so she wasn't upset by it. She heard the door slam and guessed that the men had left but a short time later she heard the door being slammed again. When the poor kid went into the room later, she found her mother's body on the floor. It was just about dusk and the kid walked into town for help.'

'How can she be a witness if she didn't know what I looked like?' asked Ben feeling saddened by what his sister had been through, but encouraged that the case against him was flimsy.

'Because,' Brewster replied, still looking uncertain, 'as Errol Carlisle explained, it's too much of a coincidence that you just show up at this time. Kelvin Carlisle had threatened to withdraw his offer if your mother didn't agree to sell by next week. I wasn't entirely convinced myself but when I saw how frightened of you that little girl was I don't think there's much doubt that she must have seen you through the window. You had one last try to presuade your mother to sell, and then either you or Lyle went back into the house and killed her. If you got an ounce of decency left in you, then you'll plead guilty and save that little girl having to take the stand.'

# 9

Mary Jane Connor had returned to her house after seeing Ben arrested, feeling sad and confused. She sat with Clarissa as the young girl sobbed herself to sleep, knowing that in just a few hours the little girl would have to attend her mother's funeral. Mary Jane had glanced back after she had fled from Ben and had seen the marshal pointing a gun at him. She was now regretting telling Errol that the rider they had seen was Ben. He had changed so much but she had recognized him and still didn't know why she hadn't blurted his name out. If anything he was even more handsome than she remembered.

She scolded herself for thinking about Ben in this way at a time like this. Mary Jane had blamed herself for Evelyn Gleason's death because if Kelvin Carlisle hadn't been so intent on buying the Gleason house as a wedding present for Errol and her, then Evelyn Gleason would still be alive and looking forward to Ben's homecoming. Why hadn't she ignored her father's orders and waited for Ben as she had always planned?

Mary Jane had become very close to Evelyn Gleason despite their differences in age and had heard Evelyn talk often about how things would improve when Ben came home. He would sort out his brother and they would develop the ranch in just the way that their father had planned. Evelyn had confided in her that money was being held in trust back East and would be available for Ben to rebuild the ranch.

No matter what Errol and the marshal thought, she knew in her own heart that Ben couldn't be involved in his mother's death. The problem was that she didn't know how to help him, especially as she knew that it would anger Errol. He had already made it clear that he didn't like the idea of her looking after Clarissa for too long after Evelyn Gleason had been buried.

Mary Jane decided to stop worrying what Errol might think and go and try and get some help for Ben. She would go and see Jack Kearney and she would see him before the funeral.

★　★　★

Jack Kearney had spent the past year trying not to be bitter at having been forced to sell his blacksmith's business to Kelvin Carlisle. A succession of droughts had badly affected the cattle business and Jack's trade had been hard hit. The recovery that followed had been too late to help Jack.

At least he had managed to secure a job for his son, Walter, who had recently returned from Nevada. Jack himself knew that he probably wouldn't have been able to work for too much longer due to the crippling rheumatism. He had led a lonely life since his wife, Margaret, had died from a heart condition just six months ago. He was still coming to terms with his grief and it would be hard attending Evelyn Gleason's funeral.

When the Gleasons had first moved to Arberstown, Jack had considered them to be snooty folk from back East but he and Margaret had eventually become good friends with them. Jack had tried his best to warn young Lyle Gleason about the company he was keeping, but when Margaret became sick he didn't see much of the boy. Jack had promised Evelyn Gleason that he would do some work on her property when his rheumatism wasn't playing up. Now it was too late. He had always been a God-fearing man but his faith had been tested of late, although he had prayed for little Clarissa more than once in recent days.

It was just a couple of hours before the funeral and Jack was struggling with buttoning his shirt around his bull-neck when Mary Jane Connor called. He was glad that she didn't have little Clarissa with her, fearing that he wouldn't be able to cope with seeing her right now. As he sat and listened to Mary Jane's account of the events and charges against Ben, his sadness increased.

'It just ain't right, Mary Jane, that a family should be dealt so much grief. It just ain't right.'

'Do you think you might be able to help Ben, Mr Kearney?' asked Mary Jane, feeling some guilt for burdening him at a time when he was still raw about his own loss.

'I'm not sure how I can, honey, but I'll try. The first thing is to go and see the marshal and make sure that the boy gets to go to his mother's funeral.'

Mary Jane hadn't thought about Ben going to the funeral and she was glad that she had gone to see Jack Kearney.

Jack Kearney's rheumatism was bad today and by the time he had completed the short journey to the marshal's office his face was grey with the pain. Jack gave Mary Jane some reassuring words as he bade her farewell. Before he asked to see Ben, Kearney enquired if the boy was going to be allowed to attend his mother's funeral. He could tell that the question troubled the marshal.

'I've been giving that a lot of thought, Jack,' Brewster sighed. 'I won't be letting him go, but hear me out. There are a lot of people who are still mighty riled up about what's happened. Not just about a woman being murdered, but also Jeb Doran. He was a popular man, as you know.'

This wasn't the answer that Jack wanted to hear and he tried once more.

'But a man has a right to attend his ma's funeral, Marshal, and from what I hear there's no case been proven against Ben. He might have killed a man all those years ago but he had good cause. Ben's not like his brother and that's a fact.'

'Your intentions are well meant, Jack,' Brewster replied sympathetically. 'But the fact is you don't know what the man in that cell is capable of. He's been in prison and mixed with all sorts of low-life, so who knows how he's turned out? But none of this really matters because I've decided that he ain't going to the funeral, and the main reason is that little girl. She's been through enough without seeing her mother's funeral upset by some crazy mob who wants to hang her brother from the nearest tree.'

Kearney sighed heavily, accepting that what the marshal had said made sense.

'Well, do me a favour and tell Ben I'll call and see him later.' Jack couldn't hide the disappointment in his voice.

Things didn't look good for Ben and Jack needed a bit more time to prepare himself before seeing him.

\* \* \*

The funeral was conducted without incident and when Marshal Brewster returned to his office he was still feeling bad about stopping Ben from attending it, even though he had done so for the right reasons. Jack Kearney returned to see Ben and the marshal relieved some of his guilt by telling Jack that he could stay with Ben for as long as he wanted. He didn't raise any objections either when he saw the basket of food that Jack had brought.

Ben's depression was lifted by the warmth of Jack's greeting. He was surprised how much Jack had aged but the muscles were still hard when he gave Ben a bear-hug. Jack's brief account of the funeral didn't mention that Clarissa had to be held by Mary Jane as the coffin was lowered into the ground.

He listened intently as Ben recounted the story from the time that he decided to escape from prison, leaving out the bits about his night with Mora and his encounter with Callow.

When Ben had finished, Kearney shook his head.

'Well I can see why the marshal might suspect you even if the evidence is flimsy. Remember the marshal doesn't know you like I do. Brewster's only been here a couple of years but he's a good lawman and he's a fair one as well.'

Ben sighed. 'I can see how it looks, but how am I going to get out of this? The marshal's probably right and I'm going to hang no matter what happens. I might as well plead guilty and spare Clarissa any further grief.'

Jack was thoughtful for a moment. He had an idea that might just help.

'Now, hold on, boy, we ain't beaten just yet. Silas Deacon is well known by folks here and although he's a bit of a rogue, he's well respected and the marshal likes him. If we can get Silas to testify that you were at his place when you said, then that'll prove you're innocent.'

Ben was heartened by Jack's suggestion but there was still a problem.

'But how are we going to get Silas here?'

'That won't be too hard,' Jack

replied, desperate to be positive. 'My Walter will go and get him. You probably don't remember Walter because he was living in Nevada while you were growing up but he did visit occasionally. Anyways, he came back to settle here and runs my old smithy. Walter won't mind going and I'm sure old Silas will use the opportunity to bring a load of whiskey to town.

'Now I'm going to explain our plans to the marshal and ask him to hold off any trial until Walter gets back with Silas. Walter will leave first thing tomorrow and he should be back before nightfall.'

By the time the old family friend left his cell Ben was much more hopeful. But before he slept that night a lot of doubts crept into his mind. He was remembering how serious Deacon had looked before he left. The old man might still be sore about what had happened between Ben and Mora and be unwilling to help him for a number of reasons.

Walter Kearney rode out of Arberstown early the following morning on a mission that he hoped would help Ben. It would be a long day in the saddle to reach Deacon's place and get back before nightfall but it would be a change for him. He only had vague memories of Ben as a boy but if his pa thought that he was innocent and needed help then that was all that mattered.

Walter had visited Deacon several times before, and was looking forward to enjoying some of the old-timer's jokes and his hospitality. But most of all he was looking forward to seeing the young Mexican woman who lived with Silas. Walter was a happily married man, but he was also a hot-blooded male and even if the stories about her were only half true she would still be worth seeing. Walter's wife Brenda was pretty and a fine wife but she wasn't the sort of woman who would get a man excited just by looking at her, especially now that she had piled on those extra pounds.

★ ★ ★

When Mora saw the rider coming towards the house she wondered if her prayers had been answered after all. Deep down she knew that a man who had enjoyed the physical pleasure that she'd given Ben would return for more. He might have reasons for not wanting to, but all men are weak when it comes to pleasures of the flesh. According to her mama a wise man does not choose to marry a woman because she is pretty or acceptable to his family or because she will make a good mother. None of these things matters compared to a woman who brings pleasure in bed. A truly wise man would be prepared to marry a woman as ugly as sin as long as she pleasures him where it matters. Mora's mama might well have gone to the same school of philosophy as Ben's friend Denny Foley.

She thanked her guardian angel for bringing Ben back because by this time tomorrow she would have left this god-forsaken place for good. But the air was filled with Mexican swear words when she saw that the rider wasn't Ben, but some great hunk of a bear whom she had no desire for. Ugliness might be acceptable to others but not to her. Not any more.

When she came out of the cabin to greet Walter, he had politely removed his hat and he was staring at the mound of earth and the makeshift cross on which hung Deacon's distinctive red and white headband.

'What you want, meester?' Mora asked as she made the sign of the cross in the direction of the mound of earth.

'I've come to see Silas but if I'm not mistaken I'm too late. Is that him?' Walter asked, pointing towards the mound, feeling uneasy.

Mora nodded and dabbed her eyes with a small handkerchief, even though they were free of tears.

'He died in bed two nights ago while we make love. I warned him about getting excited but he wouldn't listen to me.'

Walter took a hard swallow, his eyes drawn by the thrust of her breasts straining against the black dress. The stories of Mora's body hadn't been exaggerated. He felt guilty about his thoughts, particularly with the old man so fresh in his grave.

'Do you want a drink?' Mora asked.

'I'd be much obliged, ma'am, but I think I had better grab that spade and bury Silas a bit deeper.' He had noticed that one of Silas's hands was poking above the earth and it was a wonder that some wild creature hadn't shown some interest in it. The covering of soil over the body was no more than six inches. As he disturbed the soil, Walter found himself staring at the open-eyed Deacon. One thing was for sure: he hadn't gone with a smile on his face. The craggy features were contorted and there was a large bruise on one side of his temple. Walter figured it might have been caused by falling out of bed.

Walter smiled when he saw that the right arm was clasping a whiskey bottle: it made him think that Mora must have a sense of humour to go with her magnificent body. By the time she returned with the drink, Walter was just filling in the last couple of feet of earth into the deep grave.

He had been working in the hot sun and had removed his shirt. The sight of his rippling muscles that glistened with sweat had grabbed Mora's attention.

'You are a beeg man, *señor* . . . ?' she said inviting him to give his name. Suddenly she was thinking he wasn't so ugly after all.

'The name's Walter, *señorita*,' he replied, wiping his sweaty hand on his trousers and offering it to the girl. She held on to his giant-sized hand for what seemed an age. He felt uncomfortable as Mora's gaze focused on his crotch and she repeated again that he was a big man. He stuttered like a tongue-tied school-boy when Mora asked him if he would like to go inside for awhile, and told him how lonely she was. Her English wasn't perfect but he got the message that Mora wasn't grieving for Deacon and was ready to share the bed he'd died in, with a complete stranger.

Walter made his excuses about needing to get back before dark and once she'd answered a few questions about Ben, got ready to make a hasty retreat. He declined her offer of one of Deacon's bottles of home-made whiskey and as he rode off he could tell that she was none too happy. The Mexican words that she shouted after him didn't sound as though she was wishing him a safe journey.

Within minutes of Walter's departure Mora had realized that she had made a mistake in telling the big oaf that no one had called at the cabin for weeks, except the man who had stolen her horse some days ago. The big man had mentioned that Ben came from a rich family and was a good man, but this was after she had denied ever seeing him.

Mora decided that she would go into Arberstown and tell the marshal that Ben had called at the cabin and, if she had to, she could verify that she and Ben had slept together. She could supply details about Ben that would prove that she was telling the truth. It might be embarrassing for Ben but she guessed that it would be better than hanging. She had been so mad with Ben for sneaking away like he did, leaving her with the wrinkly old Deacon. He preferred to get his pleasures from a bottle, rather than her body. But now she was glad that Ben hadn't taken one of the bottles of whiskey that she had added poison to. It had taken a long time searching for the herbs and plants that she needed to make up the poison mixture that her mama had told her about. Deacon didn't have a lot of money but it would have been enough for her to get by in a big town before she met someone who would satisfy all her needs.

Perhaps now she had a chance to achieve all she wanted with Ben Gleason who would be grateful after she had saved his life. She had already packed her few belongings and just needed to empty the contents of the remaining 'doctored' whiskey bottles in case someone drank from them.

As Mora made her way to the small barn to saddle Deacon's horse she wished she had asked Walter to do it. It was something she hadn't done before, but if an old fool like Deacon could manage it then she could. But it took longer than she intended. Deacon's faithful friend wasn't used to being struck and cursed at in a strange language, and let his new rider know by kicking his hind legs out. By the time Mora emerged from the barn she wasn't looking forward to the long ride to Arberstown and she hoped that it would all be worthwhile. As she rode past Deacon's grave she turned to take one last look at the cabin and fell to the ground when the saddle slipped after the horse stumbled on the spade that was sticking out of the ground near Deacon's resting place. She didn't fall very far but landed awkwardly. She wouldn't be making the trip to Arberstown, at least not today.

# 10

When Ben saw Jack and Walter approach his cell he knew that they hadn't come with good news. Despite his own troubles Ben was saddened to hear that Deacon was dead and he asked Walter if Mora was still there. She could just as well act as a witness.

'The lying little . . . ' was all that Ben said when Walter told him that Mora had denied knowing him. Ben realized that fate had conspired to make matters worse for him because now the marshal would think that he had told more lies. He also wondered if Jack Kearney and his son really believed him after what had happened.

Jack dismissed Ben's fear. 'Of course we believe you, son.'

'I wouldn't get your hopes up, Ben,' said Walter, 'but I told Mora that your family was rich. I figured that if she's a bit of a gold-digger she might be prepared to testify on your behalf.'

Ben had a pretty good idea why Mora had been prepared to let him rot in jail or even worse, but he didn't see any point in explaining it to the Kearneys. Ben asked Jack to tell Mary Jane about what had happened, especially the part about not trusting what Mora had said. It was important to Ben that Mary Jane didn't think badly of him and, although he hoped that Mora would help him, he didn't like the idea that she would ever meet up with Mary Jane.

Marshal Brewster didn't look too pleased when he approached Ben's cell after the Kearneys had left.

'I don't know what you were hoping to prove with this business about staying with old Deacon. Now we know it was a pack of lies. I'll be sending for Judge Jardine today and I expect your trial will be next week. Perhaps you'll think on what I said about pleading guilty for your sister's sake.'

Ben could understand why the marshal was feeling angry and when the lawman left Ben slumped on to his bed feeling that his life had just about reached rock bottom.

*   *   *

Judge Giles S Jardine arrived in Arberstown the following Thursday and the trial took place the next day in the Drinking Well saloon. It would be the second time that Ben would face a possible death sentence in this room but it was a different judge this time. The interior had changed a lot, looking far grander and reflecting the town's improved prosperity and the investment of the saloon's current owner, Kelvin Carlisle.

As he glanced around the packed room he was pleased that Mary Jane wasn't there, although he recognized the round body and balding head of her father. Jack Kearney gave him a friendly nod that was in contrast to the glares and scowls of most of the others. Some of them began to mutter and one put a hand to his throat as though to indicate to Ben that he was going to hang, but the fearsome-looking Judge Jardine banged his gavel on the table and threatened to have the court cleared except for those actually taking part in the case. The judge's reputation was well known and silence descended on the gathering.

Ben held the gaze of a number of men, causing them to look away. He might have felt disheartened but he was still proud and most of all he knew that he was an innocent man. John Neville, who ran the local newspaper, had agreed to act as Ben's legal representative, but only after the persuasion of Jack Kearney.

Judge Jardine was a small wiry man who peered at Ben over his spectacles, making his dislike of Ben obvious for all to see. Any hope that the judge would be impartial was removed by his opening remarks.

'Before I commence the trial I would like to congratulate the men of Arberstown for their restraint, without which this trial would not be taking place today. I am informed that the defendant intends to plead guilty to the most hideous of crimes, that of murdering the loving mother who brought him into the world and cared for him. I am told that she even stood by him after he had murdered a man in this very room and was ready to welcome him back into her home at the end of his sentence.'

Jardine went on to inform those present that today would be the fiftieth time that he would have sentenced a man to hang. He shuffled the papers in front of him and cleared his throat before turning to face John Neville.

'Mr Neville, how does the defendant plead to the charges of murdering or conspiring to murdering Mrs Evelyn Gleason and Jeb Doran?'

'Guilty to conspiracy your honour but my client insists that he did not murder his mother, nor does he have any reason to believe that his brother did either.'

Jardine sighed, clearly upset with John Neville's presentation.

'Mr Neville, either your client is pleading guilty or not, there can be no in-between.'

'Guilty,' responded Neville who then turned to Ben with an apologetic look, feeling that he had failed to register what Ben wished to be known.

'Good, then let us get on with it. I have read your client's feeble attempts to provide himself with an alibi and I am glad that he has chosen not to waste our time.' Jardine paused briefly before reading from the notes that he had prepared. 'I must say that I have had the misfortune to try and sentence some cruel men in my time. Men who had killed others in horrific circumstances but a man who would be party to the killing of his own mother is not just cruel, he is evil.'

Within a mere seven minutes of the

court proceedings being opened, Ben had been sentenced to death by hanging. The judgment had been followed by noisy cheering from almost all those who heard it, and this time Judge Jardine did nothing to stop it.

★　★　★

It was dusk when Walter Kearney arrived back in Arberstown after a secret trip to try and save Ben's life, feeling that it had been in vain. He was on the point of collapse when his father opened the door, but he managed to ask the question that had preoccupied his thoughts during his trip back.

'Is Ben still alive?' he asked before any form of customary greeting.

'He is, son, but the hanging is scheduled for tomorrow. Sit yourself down and tell me how you got on while I get you a drink. You look done in. By the way, Brenda and the children are fine.'

'And the smithy?' Walter asked before

taking the glass from his father and gulping down the contents.

'No problems there,' Jack replied. 'It was good to be back at work and I didn't feel even a twinge from the rheumatism.'

He didn't tell his son that Errol Carlisle was none too pleased that he had taken off to attend to some family business while Jack stood in for him.

'Anyway, the important thing is, how did you get on? I had just about given up on you getting back in time. Ben has tried to keep his spirits up but he's feeling pretty low, and I was tempted to tell him about your trip to Cragoma Plains prison.'

Walter knew that his father was about to be disappointed.

'The thing is, Pa, I haven't really got any news I can tell you. We'll have to wait until I give the marshal the letter I've brought back.'

Jack looked frustrated. 'But you must have some idea what's in the letter. Did you speak to the governor and did he confirm what Ben told us?'

'Not really. He said very little. I think he understood that it was important but he seemed more interested in the fact that one of his senior guards had gone missing. Apparently it was the one who was guarding Ben when he escaped. He hasn't returned from leave. That was the only time that the governor mentioned Ben's escape.'

'Walter, he must have given you some idea,' Jack persisted, clearly upset by the lack of news and fearing the worst. Walter would have tried his best but he wasn't used to dealing with officials.

'So where's this letter?' Jack snapped at his son and immediately regretted it. 'I'm sorry son; I know you've done your best. I guess I'm feeling the strain.'

'That's all right, Pa. I understand.'

Walter unbuttoned his shirt, pulled out the crumpled envelope and handed it to his father. Jack Kearney inspected the official-looking letter. He couldn't read very well but there was no mistaking that it was addressed to the marshal and the envelope was sealed with some kind of fancy crest. Jack yanked the chain that held his watch in his breast pocket and squinted at the large face.

'Ten o'clock! I wonder if the marshal is still at his office. We could have a scout around town for him or catch him at home. Not that he's there very often, him being a single man. No, on second thoughts, we'll wait until first thing in the morning. I'll be praying that your trip was a success, son. I sure appreciate you trying. Now I expect you'll want to get home. I'll call for you at about eight o'clock in the morning. We'll be at the marshal's office waiting for him.'

Jack patted his son's shoulder and wished him good-night.

When it got to three in the morning and Jack still hadn't managed to get to sleep, he was regretting not showing the letter to the marshal the night before. At six o'clock he ceased trying to sleep and got up. If his reading skills had been better, he would have been tempted to open the letter by now, but he knew that breaking the seal wouldn't have been a good idea.

The rain was dripping off Jack's hat by the time he reached Walter's house and then they trudged their way along muddy Main Street towards the marshal's office. Neither man spoke, both occupied with their thoughts. Walter had grown to like Ben in the short time that they had become acquainted and he knew just how important helping Ben was to his pa. Father and son had their heads turned to shield themselves against the driving rain and reached the steps of what had been the marshal's office — but was now a burnt-out shell.

They had just stepped up on to the badly scorched porch when Marshal Brewster called out from behind them.

'Don't worry, Jack. He's injured some but he's still alive and over at Doc Sloane's. There's a meeting later to decide whether to go ahead with the hanging. What with the weather and all.

matter what sort of state he's in.'

'How bad is he and how did it happen?' Walter asked.

'It's his hands mainly and his chest where his clothes caught fire. He'd be dead now if it wasn't for Errol Carlisle helping to pull him out. I don't know how it started but I think it's a fair bet that someone didn't want to wait for the hanging. There was a lot of straw near the porch and around the back.'

'Can we go and see him, Marshal? Jack asked. 'We'd like you to come with us because we've got something really important to show you.'

Ben was still sleeping when they arrived. Doctor Sloane suggested that they could wait until he woke up, or come back later. Jack opted to wait and was soon handing Marshal Brewster the letter. The tension was high as Jack and Walter watched the lawman tear it open and start to read, but it was to get worse when the grim faced marshal said he had things to do relating to the hanging and couldn't discuss the letter. His parting comment before he left was that all would be revealed at the meeting he was going to arrange.

Within minutes of the marshal leaving, Ben awoke. Jack was about to explain about Walter's trip when John Neville arrived. Jack's hopes that Neville had brought some news about the contents of the letter were soon dashed when Neville told Ben that the hanging had been delayed for two days to give him the chance to recover from the fire. Ben responded with a weak smile. It seemed crazy that anybody should be concerned that he was fit enough to hang.

Jack said that he would call back later, figuring that Ben would like to be on his own for a while. It would give Jack the chance to find the marshal and demand to know what was in the letter. This time he wouldn't be fobbed off.

The marshal was in the diner doing his best to demolish a giant helping of eggs and beans when Jack found him.

He paused to tell Jack that he couldn't reveal the exact contents of the letter. However, it might contain some good news but it was too early to say.

So it was nearly two hours later when Jack and Walter attended the hastily arranged meeting of the town council in the Drinking Well, ready to listen to John Neville reveal the actual contents of the letter.

'Gentlemen,' Neville began as he addressed the packed assembly of townsfolk, 'thanks to Jack and Walter Kearney a grave injustice has been prevented and we have been stopped from hanging an innocent man. Ben Gleason is completely innocent of all charges.' It was some minutes before the noisy reaction quietened down and Neville was able to continue. 'Marshal Brewster has received a letter from the governor of Cragoma Plains prison confirming that Ben could not have been in Arberstown at the time of his brother's escape or the murder of his mother. The governor also confirmed that Ben Gleason has now completed his prison sentence and is a free man. I am sure that everyone will wish Ben a speedy recovery from last night's deliberate fire. Thank you.'

Jack Kearney hugged his son with joy, while most of those around him were shocked and bewildered. Marshal Brewster came over and shook Walter and Jack by the hand, congratulating them.

'John Neville should have mentioned that Judge Jardine will have to come back in a few days and formally discharge Ben, but I have been in touch by telegraph and it will just be a formality. Now I think you men will want to get over to the doc's house and pass on the good news.'

\* \* \*

Three days after the dramatic news Ben was well enough to move to Jack Kearney's house. He was preparing to leave, when Dr Sloane came back from a visit to William Connor's and asked him a question that caused him some fresh concern.

'Ben, do you know a young Mexican girl named Mora who was living with Silas Deacon?'

'I met her once at Deacon's place. Why do you ask?' Ben was surprised and concerned by the doc's enquiry.

'I had an idea that you must have met her when you stayed at Deacon's, that's all. I've just seen her over at Connor's and Mary Jane is very upset.'

Ben was quietly cursing his luck and worrying that Mora could ruin his chances with Mary Jane at a time when, according to Walter Kearney, she was on the verge of calling off her engagement to Errol. Ben was so preoccupied that he hadn't heard the doc explain that Mora must have been a nice looking girl and that it had been a shock for those who had found her and brought her back to William Connor's.

Ben had come out of his thoughts in

time to hear Doc Sloane say:

'It looks as though she must have died from a broken neck, probably from a fall rather than anything else. There must be a jinx on that old place of Deacon's. First there was old Silas and then last week Luke Bradley found the naked body of a man who had died from drinking some of Deacon's poisoned whiskey, and now that poor girl.'

Ben was shocked to hear about the fate of Mora but he was interested in the man who had been brought in and asked the doctor how he knew that the man had died from poisoning and that it was the result of Deacon's whiskey.

'Well, he had two empty bottles of 'Deacon's Specials' beside him and the colour of his skin left me in no doubt that he was poisoned. Luke Bradley also told me that the spot where he found the body was covered with dead rats. I'm not sure if the rats were partial to Deacon's whiskey or if they had eaten the dead man's poisoned flesh, but judging by the state of the body, I would say it was the latter.'

Ben was tempted to ask exactly where the body had been found, but he wasn't in much doubt that it must have been Lucas Callow. Ben hadn't taken any notice of the label on the whiskey bottles but they must have been supplied by Deacon. It left Ben thinking that he had to thank the late Silas Deacon for more than his night of passion with Mora. Ben would never know that it was the Mexican girl who had inadvertently saved his life and not old Silas.

★   ★   ★

Within three weeks Ben had fully recovered and he had been grateful for the frequent visits from Mary Jane and Clarissa, especially when they brought him some samples of Ma Connor's cooking. Ben didn't like to pry but he could tell from little things that were said that Mary Jane and Errol's relationship was under a great strain and he hoped that it would soon collapse. Clarissa didn't say much about Errol but it was obvious that she didn't like him.

# 11

Marshal Brewster was still feeling guilty about his involvement in falsely accusing Ben and knew that he shouldn't have allowed himself to be influenced by Errol Carlisle. He had visited Ben a number of times whilst he was recovering and he believed Ben's vow to track down his brother and return him to face the consequences. So the marshal figured that he was doing Ben a favour when he told him that his brother had been seen two weeks ago in Harpers Post. Harpers Post didn't have a marshal but, despite being much smaller than Arberstown, it was served by the railroad.

It was the very news that Ben had awaited, knowing that his life would be on hold until he had found his mother's killer — and that meant finding his brother.

When Ben met Clarissa and Mary Jane outside the Connor's the following day he told Clarissa that he was going away on some legal business. He was taken aback when he saw the tears in her eyes as she broke away from his hug and ran towards the house.

After he told Mary Jane the real reason that he was going away she seemed concerned for his safety. He sensed that her anxiety was greater than that normally reserved for a friend and he felt her tremble as he hugged her briefly, wishing that he could have told her how he felt about her.

Mary Jane was still in Ben's thoughts by the time he had completed half of the journey to Harpers Post and if he hadn't been so preoccupied he would have seen how the scenery had changed. The lush pastures had been replaced by a dusty wilderness and the land was flat for as far as the eye could see. He would soon become anxious about finding some water for his mount as the temperature was noticeably higher away from the mountains west of Arberstown. The marshal had said that his informant had seen Lyle spending a lot of money; he was clearly enjoying life on the run.

As he rode, Ben considered the question that had plagued him for most of the previous night. Would he shoot Lyle if he discovered that he had killed their mother? After all he had killed his father's murderer so why not his mother's.

It was early afternoon when he arrived at the outskirts of Harpers Post and he felt a strange unease about the place. By the time he reached Main Street he didn't feel any better. Perhaps it might have been a thriving town once but everything about the place now gave an impression of neglect. All the buildings were on the one side of the street except for a large hotel which was in front of the railroad depot. Judging by the number of horses tied to the hitch rail outside the run-down saloon, most of the town's menfolk must be crowded inside. Ben decided against squeezing his animal alongside the others. Instead, he led it to the empty rail outside the store, which had a very badly written sign. Whoever had painted 'Joe's Place' was no artist and must have had a serious bout of the shakes at the time.

In contrast to the Drinking Well, Harpers Post's only saloon appeared tiny with a bar no more than twelve feet long. Ben couldn't see how Lyle or anyone else could have had fun in this hell-hole. None of the men standing at or near the bar paid him much attention as he found a small gap between the assembled bodies. In contrast to his customers, the barman, a short man with a full grey beard and very dark hair, obviously dyed, was positively jovial.

'Howdy, mister. What'll your poison be? By the way the drinks are on the house today, on account of it being a very special occasion.'

Ben was reminded of Callow as he

replied, 'Beer would be fine.' He was thinking that the free drinks might account for the state of the men alongside him. Apart from a few recent visits to the Drinking Well with Jack and Walter Kearney he had no experience of saloons and he wondered if this one was more typical of them than the Drinking Well.

The barman landed the beer in front of him, causing some of it to spill on the counter, adding to the river of liquid. On closer inspection it was obvious that the barman had probably been drinking as much as his customers.

'By the way, the free drinks offer only applies in here and not the main bar through that door,' advised the barman. 'You might want to go there later if you're looking for some company. I mean female company, as in a nice-looking filly that likes to give a man what he wants most.'

Ben didn't respond but he was thinking that the other bar might be where Lyle had his fun.

'Anyway, what brings you to our little paradise in the wilderness? We haven't had a train in here for a week, so I guess you came on the back of one of those four-legged things.'

Ben didn't see any reason to be secretive. He wouldn't find Lyle that way so he told the inquisitive barman that he was looking for his brother.

'Then you've come to the right place, because if he's in town, then I'll know him. They don't call me Nosy Johnson for nothing. What's his name?' The barman turned to the locals for some sort of acknowledgement, but they ignored him.

'His name's Lyle Gleason,' Ben replied, keeping his voice low.

The grin disappeared from the barman's face and the whole gathering turned towards Ben, leaving him in no doubt that he had come to the right place and that there was nothing wrong with their ears.

'Lyle's a kind of unusual name. I

don't suppose there can be many of them around,' said the barman, obviously conscious that the gathering was interested in his words.

'So you wouldn't forget him, then?' said Ben sensing that something was wrong as the chatty barman had suddenly become defensive.

'No. I wouldn't forget a name like that. Look, why don't I show you next door? It's closed right now but you might want to come back tonight when the place comes alive.'

The barman didn't wait for a response but lifted a hinged section of the bar and came around to Ben's side. Whatever the barman was up to, it obviously had something to do with Lyle so Ben followed him through the door. In contrast to the front bar the room was massive, not quite as grand as the one in Arberstown but still quite impressive.

'The other bar is where the serious drinking is done but this is what you might call the fun place, with plenty of gambling and some beautiful girls. Let's sit down for a while and get acquainted. I'll get you another drink if you like. It'll be free, of course.'

Ben declined but the barman helped himself to a large glass of whiskey and then rejoined him at the table.

'Is this where my brother comes?' Ben asked. He was already convinced that the barman knew Lyle.

The barman took his second large gulp of whiskey.

'Are you and your brother what you might call close?'

'We could be, but I haven't seen him for nigh on seven years,' Ben replied.

'Look, mister. There ain't no easy way to tell you this, but we buried Lyle no more than an hour ago. Some of those men back there carried his coffin. The free drinking today is being paid for with Lyle's leftover money after his funeral expenses. I'm real sorry because he was well liked around here.'

According to what the barman told him, Ben calculated that Lyle must have arrived soon after the time of his escape in Arberstown and he was alone. He had been staying at the hotel opposite with one of the saloon girls. Two nights ago he got involved in an argument during a card game just a few tables away from where they were now sitting. It seemed that he had falsely accused someone of cheating and pulled a knife on the man, guns weren't allowed at the tables. He ended up being stabbed to death with his own knife. The fella that did it left town just after it happened, but everyone agreed he'd acted in self-defence. Lyle had been drinking heavily before the game and there was no reasoning with him. No one knew where he came from, so that was why they used what was left of his money to supply free drinks. They figured he was a fun-loving guy who would have approved of such an arrangement.

The barman offered to give Ben whatever was left of the proceeds and told him that Lyle's horse was at the blacksmith's. Ben told him that he would take the horse but they could keep the money that was left over.

Ben left the saloon and made his way to the small cemetery on the outskirts of the town. The freshly dug grave had a single bunch of wild flowers with a note attached that read *We'll miss you, Lyle — Love, Dorothy, Michelle and Leah*.

Ben felt dead inside, unable to feel any emotion for a brother who, it seemed, had killed their mother. Now, Ben would never know for certain.

He thought of staying the night and talking with Lyle's girl. It would be easy enough to find out if it was Dorothy, Michelle or Leah. It was unlikely that Lyle would have confessed to the girl and Ben decided to head back to Arberstown, planning to sleep out in the open if he couldn't make it by dark. So, once he had picked up some food at Joe's Place and Lyle's horse from the blacksmith's he was starting the journey home much sooner than expected.

Lyle's death had thrown him and he would always wonder what had really happened the day his mother was murdered, but by the time he had reached home he was determined that he wouldn't let it ruin his life. The ride had been uneventful and he had made good time by switching between the horses. The light had only just started fading by the time he reached the Gleason house.

The following morning Ben was up early and set about replacing some of the rotten wood on the porch. He was still determined to restore the house to its former glory, knowing that this was what his mother would have wanted.

He was finishing work for the day when Jack Kearney arrived with some more supplies. Jack was surprised to see Ben and shocked as he listened to the account of what he had discovered in Harpers Post. Jack put a hand on Ben's shoulder.

'Perhaps it's the best thing that could have happened, son. All right, there are still a few unanswered questions but at least you were spared having to kill your own brother.'

'I still can't get it into my head that Lyle could have turned out the way he did. If only Ma had told me!'

Jack knew that Ben would agonize over this for a long, long time. He might think things had been settled but Jack had his doubts whether it was going to be that easy. He decided to change the subject, hoping it would help Ben.

'I see you bought yourself a new horse. Are you planning on doing a bit of breeding?' He nodded towards the corral.

'No, that's Lyle's horse. I don't know why I brought it back. It will only be another reminder. You or Walter can have it or sell it on.'

'That's not Lyle's horse. He wouldn't have been seen riding on a plain old horse like that, or either of those saddles there. Lyle had a black stallion and a real fancy saddle. He had it custom-made by a St Louis saddle-maker who was doing some work for the Carlisles. I reckon Lyle was trying to outdo Errol. It was a modified Plains saddle with a double cinch. It had lots of fancy metal studs mounted in the strapping. But that old grey does look kind of familiar. Let's go and have a closer look.'

When they reached the corral Jack picked up some straw and the two horses galloped over towards them.

'I thought so,' Jack commented. 'See that brand. That's a Carlisle horse. Carlisle provides for all his men from his own breeding stock and they're all good quality animals.'

'Lyle must have stolen it,' Ben said. 'Perhaps Walter wouldn't mind handing it over to one of Carlisle's men.'

'Walter will take care of it for you, but I don't think Lyle stole the animal. When Lyle was arrested the marshal asked Walter to look after Lyle's horse until things were sorted out. On the night that Lyle escaped his horse and saddle was taken from the stable at the back of Walter's smithy.'

'And you think that Lyle escaped using his own horse?'

'Well, if he didn't, then it was a mighty coincidence,' Jack replied. 'Perhaps he swapped it with one of Carlisle's men and got a bit of extra cash thrown in. That would explain why he was able to throw his money about in Harpers Post.'

Ben couldn't make sense of this; now that Lyle was dead perhaps it shouldn't matter to him, but it did, and Jack could see that he was troubled by his explanation.

'You'd best forget what happened with the horse, son,' Jack said. 'Try and put all this behind you and start looking at the future for you and Clarissa. I saw her yesterday and she really is a sweet young thing.' Jack saved the news that would please Ben until the last. 'I was also speaking to William Connor yesterday and he told me that Mary Jane has broken off the engagement to the Carlisle boy. William didn't seem upset about it. It could be because Errol is about as popular as his old man.'

Ben was pleased about the news that Mary Jane had finished with Carlisle, but as he watched Jack leave with the old grey tied behind his wagon, he couldn't let matters rest. He intended to go and see the marshal. Perhaps Marshal Brewster could shed some light on the mystery surrounding Lyle's horse.

# 12

Marshal Brewster was surprised when he heard Ben's account of what he had discovered in Harpers Post. The recent deaths had created a lot of upset and tension in the town and he hoped that the news of Lyle Gleason's demise would help get things back to normal.

'I hope that this is the end of the matter, Ben, but there are going to be some folks who will say that you have made up this story to get the case closed. Others like me know how determined you were to get justice for what happened to your ma.'

Ben shrugged his shoulders. 'I suppose some folks will think that way, but with Lyle dead I guess we'll never know what really happened.'

The marshal couldn't explain the mystery of the Carlisle horse or how Lyle would have had so much money and there still remained the unanswered question of who had helped Lyle escape.

'Could one of Carlisle's men have been involved with Lyle's escape?' Ben asked.

Brewster gave a deep sigh. 'It's possible I suppose, because someone must have helped him.'

Something had been niggling Ben and he decided to test it on the marshal.

'I keep thinking that Ma's death must have had something to do with her refusing to sell the house and land to Kelvin Carlisle. I'm sure of that because nothing else makes sense.'

'Even if that were so, it doesn't help us none,' replied the marshal.

'I'm told that Lyle and Errol Carlisle were close friends and it's common knowledge that the Carlisles were pretty desperate to get my mother to sell. The man whom Clarissa saw with Lyle at the house that day could have been Errol Carlisle.'

Brewster shook his head. 'I don't much like Errol despite what you might have thought, but I don't see how he would get involved. He's not one for getting his hands dirty, nor is his father.'

Ben still hadn't changed his mind about Errol, even though he had rescued him from the fire. In Ben's experience his first impression of folks usually didn't change.

'I'd better be getting on then, Marshal. I just thought that you would like to know about Lyle.'

'Just before you go, Ben, I have a proposition I'd like you to think over.'

The marshal's proposal was almost as surprising as finding out that his brother was dead, and he rejected it out of hand, but Brewster was persuasive and by the time Ben had left the office he had changed his mind.

★　★　★

It was early afternoon when Ben made his way up the path to the Connors' house but before he could reach the door Clarissa came running to greet him with a hug. By the time she broke loose and he turned towards Mary Jane he had a lump in his throat.

'Ben, why are you wearing that shiny badge?' Clarissa asked.

Ben smiled. 'Because Marshal Brewster's made me his deputy, honey.'

Mary Jane couldn't hide her surprise.

'Deputy?' She gave him a quizzical smile.

Ben returned her smile. 'It's a long story. I'll tell you about it later.'

He had brought his young sister a skipping-rope and she pleaded with him to take her and Mary Jane for a walk so that she could try it out. The change in Clarissa was dramatic and he knew that credit for that should go to Mary Jane. He told her so as he watched Clarissa skip in front of them. When he raised the subject of her split with Errol she didn't appear too upset as she explained that the relationship had been under a lot of strain. She told Ben that it had nothing to do with her involvement with Clarissa or the Gleasons, but Ben wasn't convinced.

Mary Jane was close to tears when he told her about Lyle, realizing that it could only have added to Ben's sorrow. She agreed that it would be best not to tell Clarissa the news for the time being.

Mary Jane looked troubled when she asked him about working for the marshal and he tried to reassure her.

'I know that some folks will question whether I should be doing it because of my past, but Marshal Brewster is confident that he can handle the doubters. The job's only part-time and I'll still be able to work on the house. The main reason I took the job, Mary Jane, is that it might just help me get accepted by folks and maybe restore the family name.'

She smiled but she was still troubled. 'Please be careful, Ben.'

The following day an official-looking letter addressed to Ben c/o Jack Kearney arrived. The contents explained that an interim sum of money had been transferred to an account set up in his name at the bank in Arberstown. A representative of the legal firm would be visiting Arberstown to discuss the contents of his mother's will, but the main feature was that he and Clarissa were to be equal beneficiaries of a very large estate.

The news of the money meant that he could buy the materials that he needed for refurbishment of the house. Ben spent his spare time working on it with the help of Jack Kearney.

During various talks with Jack, the marshal and others, he had built up a picture of his brother. He discovered that Lyle had made his mother's life hell during the last year through his gambling and lying, but they had apparently remained very close.

\* \* \*

Within a couple of months the Gleason house repairs were nearing completion. Ben and Jack had taken to staying overnight so that they could spend longer getting on with the work. He intended to make sure that the house would be as bright, warm and friendly as it had been when he was a boy. It would bear no resemblance to the run-down place that Clarissa had fled from screaming, after discovering her mother's body.

During his nightly patrols of the Drinking Well Ben noticed that Errol Carlisle was usually fired up with drink. Carlisle would always be accompanied by men who worked on the Carlisle ranch and he would often belittle them, knowing that they would not retaliate for fear of losing their jobs, as well as nights out at Errol's expense. Ben had been on the point of arresting him on a few occasions but Carlisle always backed off at the last moment, but not so on the night that Errol was celebrating his birthday. Errol was buying everyone a drink to celebrate the occasion. Some of his so called 'friends' were having difficulty standing up but they seemed to be in good humour. By comparison Errol looked cold sober and morose as he glared at Ben. There was no doubting the malice when he addressed Ben.

'It's the killer deputy. How are you getting on with my cast-off, frigid Mary Jane? Is she still as cold as one of her old man's dead clients?'

The bar was filled with the forced laughter from Errol's entourage, most of whom hated his guts but as long as he was buying the drinks they would laugh to order.

Ben had been well schooled by Marshal Brewster and refused to be baited by Carlisle. He smiled when he told Errol to enjoy his birthday and then he started to walk away.

Carlisle was too fired up to let it end there.

'Take it from me,' he announced, 'Mary Jane's a real cold fish, not like your mother, deputy boy. I hear that she was always real hot for it, entertaining all those men up at that big house after your weakling of a pa got what he deserved.'

The laughter stopped when Ben rounded on Carlisle and head-butted him full on the nose, sending him reeling into two of his drinking companions. Some of the blood from Carlisle's shattered nose sprayed across the bar and into the drinking glasses, colouring the beer. Ben moved his left hand closer to his pistol. He glared at the group of Carlisle's men as though inviting them to make a move. Perhaps they reminded themselves that Ben had killed before and probably wouldn't hesitate to do it again. Two of the men who had been sent sprawling by the falling Carlisle helped him to his feet and he struggled to keep his balance, still affected by the blow.

'Now I would suggest that you take your foul, loud-mouthed friend home to his daddy,' Ben ordered, 'before someone really gets hurt, and I mean much more than a busted nose.'

Ben was still scanning the group in

front of him when one of Carlisle's men who had been playing cards came up behind him, drew his pistol and pressed it into Ben's back.

'Well done, Jacko. Take his gun away from him and then perhaps we can have some fun with the big man here,' Carlisle sneered as he stood unsupported and seemingly recovered from Ben's assault.

After Ben had dropped his gun to the floor, Carlisle ordered two of his men to hold Ben, then he stepped forward and delivered two vicious punches into his stomach. As Ben slumped from the effects of the blows Carlisle pistol-whipped him across the side of his face.

Carlisle was about to deliver another blow with his pistol when he halted with the weapon in mid-air.

'I've got an idea that will give us some real fun,' he said, lowering the pistol. 'Jacko, take his belt off and replace it with yours.'

Jacko looked puzzled but he placed his own gun on the bar and then carried out Carlisle's instructions.

Carlisle smiled as he ordered Jacko to raise Ben's right hand in the air, telling him to force Ben's fingers open. 'As you can see, boys, our friend has no trigger finger on his right hand. I figure him being a convicted killer should just about even things up during the little showdown that him and me are about to have.'

Jerry, the head barman, could see that he was about to witness cold-blooded murder. He had to try to prevent it.

'Come on, Errol. Why don't you stop this now?' he cried out. 'We can all see you've got the better of him. He caught you off guard but that cracked cheek-bone of his won't heal in a hurry. I bet he'll be marked for life.'

Carlisle rounded on the barman and for a moment it looked as though he was going to shoot him.

'Shut your great fat mouth, you beer-swilling ape. Open it once more and you'll never work in this town again. Jacko, put a gun in Gleason's holster.'

Carlisle turned to face Ben.

'Gleason,' he snarled, 'I think you'll die here tonight, but I'm going to give you a chance by letting you draw first. It's not much of a chance, but you might get lucky. Now if you don't want to take it then I'll just shoot you and everyone will swear that you went for your weapon first. Isn't that right, boys?'

There was a chorus of acknowledgements from all around Carlisle, although some of them were beginning to feel sick at the thought that any moment now Gleason would be killed right before their eyes.

Ben just smiled back. 'I don't suppose you've ever had the guts to shoot an able-bodied man face to face, Carlisle. Well, I have and that's because I haven't got a yellow streak down my back like you. Perhaps you think I'm going to squeal for mercy because you know that's what you would do. That's why Mary Jane is with me now and not you. It's because she prefers a real man to a coward.'

Carlisle's rage had been boiling and he went for his gun, but before he could reach it Ben had crossed his left hand over to draw his own gun. His bullet hit Carlisle between the eyes and sent him sprawling into his men once again. But this time he was dead before he hit the floor. The draw had been possible because Jacko had holstered the gun with the handle facing forward, perhaps thinking that it didn't really matter, but he had made a mistake.

In prison, the friends of Makin had hacked off what they thought was his trigger finger, not realizing that Ben was actually left-handed.

Some of those men who had been laughing at Ben just a short while ago were sick, one of them puking over the bloodied face of Carlisle. None of those present had any thought of confronting Ben and when he waved his pistol towards the door they made a hasty retreat.

Only Jacko rode in the direction of the Carlisle ranch. The others decided to head for Harpers Post because there would be no fun working for that slave-driver Kelvin Carlisle now that their meal ticket was dead.

# 13

When Kelvin Carlisle heard the news of his son's death he swiped his hand across the oak sideboard, sending his prize collection of ceramic antiques crashing on to the hard wooden floor. That single act had destroyed a collection that had taken twenty years and countless trips to Europe to collect. He slumped forward on to the empty top of the sideboard and sobbed like a baby. The son that he idolized and had built an empire for would not inherit it now. Sol Ackroyd, the man who had brought Carlisle the news, waited in silence for nearly ten minutes before Kelvin Carlisle stood up from the sideboard and spoke to him.

'I want you to send someone into Arberstown right now and bring my son home. I want you to make sure that William Connor and none of his family so much as look at my son. Send someone to Harpers Post tonight and bring back an undertaker. I don't care what it costs, just bring him here, drag him out of bed if necessary but make sure that he is here by tomorrow. Now I want to be alone and if anyone so much as calls my name or knocks on that door I'll fire a bullet through it. Is all that absolutely clear?'

'Yes, Mr Carlisle, now don't you worry.'

Carlisle glared at Ackroyd for his audacity in offering him sympathy and flicked his hand in a gesture of dismissal.

By the time that Kelvin Carlisle had finished most of the large bottle of brandy he hated all those connected with his son's murderer. Yes, murderer, for that is what Ben Gleason was. His son had been no match for him. But it wasn't just Ben Gleason that was to blame; it was the Connors, and that bitch, Mary Jane. If she hadn't rejected his son, he wouldn't have been drinking so heavily and he would still be alive.

Well, he had plans for them all and he would make them pay for what had happened. William Connor could say goodbye to his business for starters. After the undertaker from Harpers Post had buried his son, Carlisle would make him an offer that he couldn't refuse. He would build him premises next to Connor's and if necessary subsidize it so that he could offer to bury people for free. He would drive the Connors out of Arberstown and make sure that they could never set up a business anywhere else unless they were a long, long way from here. Little Miss Clarissa was about to lose her new-found brother who was going to receive some very special treatment and would soon be joining his stubborn mother.

When Carlisle emerged from his study he roared for someone to fetch Sol Ackroyd who, upon his arrival back in Carlisle's study, was handed a list of instructions by Carlisle. He was to order black suits for the men to wear at the funeral. If Samuel Golding, the tailor, couldn't have them ready for the funeral the day after tomorrow then he could consider his lease cancelled with immediate effect. Ackroyd was also told to arrange for seven black horses and carriages for the mourners and if necessary he was to steal them.

★   ★   ★

Ben had taken Mary Jane and Clarissa for a picnic on the hill overlooking Arberstown on the day of Errol Carlisle's funeral. He left them for a short while so that he could walk to the ridge. When he looked down he saw the funeral procession snake its way from the church, heading out to the Carlisle ranch where Errol was to be buried.

Ben had been advised by the marshal to stay out of town until tomorrow and not to go near the Gleason house, but he didn't like the idea of staying away. It meant leaving the marshal to face any trouble by himself. Ben would escort Mary Jane and Clarissa to the edge of town after the picnic, then return to the hill and spend the night out in the open. It would give him the chance to do some serious thinking about his future.

★   ★   ★

Marshal Brewster wasn't too surprised when Kelvin Carlisle made a rare visit to town shortly after the funeral was over and demanded that the marshal arrest his son's killer so that he could be tried and hanged. The marshal tried to tell the grieving Carlisle as gently as he could that Errol had provoked Ben and had actually tried to draw his weapon first. Carlisle threatened to inflict his own form of justice if the law wouldn't hang Gleason. Brewster didn't bother to caution Carlisle about taking the law into his own hands. He hoped that Carlisle might reflect on things and let matters rest.

Any thoughts that things might settle down disappeared from the marshal's mind when he discovered that Carlisle had given most of his massive workforce the day off after the funeral and arranged for them to have free drinks at the saloon. Carlisle said that it was to be a 'celebration' of his son's life but for the marshal it could only spell trouble for him and Ben. He would have been even more concerned had he heard Kelvin Carlisle's speech at the funeral, where he had made it clear that it would please him if something untoward was to happen to his son's killer. Carlisle was too shrewd to actually offer a reward but his words would have the same effect on men fuelled by drink.

★　★　★

By the time that Ben made his way back down the hill the following day he had come to a few decisions, but some of them were to be discarded when he saw the weak plume of smoke that rose from the smouldering frame of the Gleason house. Whatever had happened there last night it was too late to save anything so he headed straight for town and the marshal's office.

Main Street showed no signs that there had been trouble in town the night before, but upon entering the marshal's office the stench that greeted him meant that the cells were full.

Marshal Brewster was resting his head on the desk but looked up, his face showing that he must have had a hell of a night. The blackened skin and the redness of his eyes told Ben that the marshal already knew about the fire at the Gleason house.

Ben interrupted the marshal when he started to relate the bad news.

'I already know about my place, Marshal,' he said, trying to hide the anger that he felt. 'I saw it on my way down from the hills. It looks as though it's completely destroyed. You must have had quite a night of it here in town!'

Brewster lowered his head. 'Things weren't too bad here, Ben, but I've got some really bad news about Jack Kearney. Jack had gone to do some work at the house and must have decided to stay over. I'm afraid Jack's dead. He managed to get out but the smoke must have got to him.'

Ben was numbed by the news at first, but then the anger he'd been trying to keep in check erupted. He went to the cabinet containing the rifles. He ignored the marshal's calls for him to calm down as he loaded shells into a rifle.

'Marshal, we both know that this was Carlisle's doing. Do you think any of that lot might have been involved?' Ben nodded his head in the direction of the cells.

'Ben, those men in there didn't leave town and that's a fact. I know it looks bad but it might have been an accident. I didn't want to say anything to Walter because he's devastated but you know what Jack was like with that old pipe hanging out of his mouth. I'm not saying it wasn't some of Carlisle's men, but why don't you go and see Walter? He'd appreciate that. Go and look around your house later to see if you can find any clues and then come and talk to me again.' Brewster put a friendly hand on Ben's shoulder. 'Why don't you do that, son?'

Ben knew that the marshal was offering him good advice. He placed the rifle on the desk, then walked over to the cells and glared at the occupants who were awake. He would follow the marshal's suggestion and go and see Walter Kearney.

Ben had never seen any man cry before. He'd heard them in prison but never seen anyone face to face. In between sobs, Walter vowed never to work for Carlisle again. He dismissed any idea that it was Ben's fault as he recalled how his pa had been given a new lease of life working on the property and although Ben had paid him well he would have done it for nothing.

Walter's wife had gone to pick some flowers but had asked Ben to stay until she came back because Walter couldn't cope with folks calling to sympathize. It was just as well he had because when Ben opened the door to the first caller, it was Sol Ackroyd, Carlisle's head man. Ben closed the door behind him and frog-marched Ackroyd away from the house.

'I don't know why you're here, but if Walter sees you then they'll be carrying you over to Doc Sloane's. Now move.'

'There's no need for the rough stuff. I'm only here to offer Mr Carlisle's condolences,' Ackroyd explained, wishing that he had stayed away and lied to Carlisle about delivering the message.

It took every ounce of self-control for Ben to stop himself from smashing his fist into Ackroyd's face. He might only be the messenger but he was on Carlisle business and that made him low life.

'Now you tell Carlisle that Walter doesn't want his condolences. And tell him from me that if I find out that Jack

Kearney's death was caused by one of his men then I'll make sure that he hangs. Now go and crawl back to your master.'

Ben gave Ackroyd a final push that sent him crashing to the ground. He hovered over him, hoping that the slimy messenger would think about going for his gun. Ben didn't want to kill Ackroyd but he would dearly like to send him to prison which is where he would go if he pulled a weapon on an officer of the law. But Ackroyd had no intention of endangering his life or risking his liberty. He had done what he was paid for and now he retreated as fast as he could. He wouldn't be passing on Ben's threats and making matters any worse than they already were.

Later that day Ben visited the remains of the house and searched through the rubble and round about. But he could find no evidence that the house had been set on fire deliberately. Before he left he visited the spot where his parents were buried and vowed to them that he would rebuild their home.

The mourners at Jack's funeral far outnumbered those at the recent funeral of Errol Carlisle and all of them were there because they wanted to be and not because they had been ordered or bribed.

The words of the minister struck a cord with those gathered when he said:

'Jack Kearney had never been wealthy or powerful but he was loved. He was the biggest of men with a heart to match. He knew the proper value of life and the importance of friendship, love and of the family. We can pay no greater tribute to Jack than to say that he will be sadly missed by us all and Arberstown will be a poorer place without him.'

Ben had put aside his bitterness on this sad day but he had not lost his resolve to make someone pay for Jack's untimely death. Jack had become a second father to him and

Ben would see that justice was done. He would not let the big man down. But whatever action Ben took it would be in accordance with the law this time.

# 14

It was just after three o'clock when Ben checked in at the marshal's office, it being the first time since the incident in which he had killed Errol Carlisle. He had arranged to have a meeting with the marshal so he was surprised to find that the office was empty. The note on the desk explained that Brewster had been called away to an incident at the Carlisle ranch, and he wanted Ben to hold the fort.

In the quiet of the office Ben had time to reflect on his feelings towards Mary Jane. She had told him about Carlisle's plans to drive her pa out of business, which would force the family to leave the area. Ben had decided that he couldn't let her go without making her aware of his true feelings for her: the same feelings that he had had towards her and was about to declare when the tragic events separated them years ago. He was certain she had reciprocal feelings and he remembered the trust she had shown towards him when he had first arrived back in Arberstown. He would wait just a little while longer in the hope that some matters could be settled but before the month was out he would ask her to marry him.

Ben was debating whether to do a patrol of the town, but he hadn't been sleeping too well of late and was dozing at the desk when Sol Ackroyd burst into the office. Ackroyd blurted out something about Lyle causing trouble over at the saloon and disappeared out of the door before Ben could question him.

Ben swilled his face with water from the bowl, gathered his thoughts and pondered what he had just been told. It had to be some kind of a set-up or a sick joke because by now everyone knew that his brother was dead. It also seemed an odd coincidence that the marshal had been called away to the

Carlisle ranch. The sensible thing would be to wait for the marshal but Ben would take his chances by himself.

He checked his weapon as he made the short trip across the street but faltered when he saw the black stallion tied to the hitch rail. The beautiful animal with the fancy saddle was certainly like the horse that Jack had described as Lyle's and Ben wondered if it now belonged to Ackroyd. Everything looked and felt normal in the saloon for this time of day. The three men sitting at the card table were known to Ben and wouldn't be involved in any trouble. Ackroyd was positioned to the left of the man who might be part of the set-up. It was possible that he was a hired gun brought in by Kelvin Carlisle and Ben was thinking that he should have ignored Ackroyd and let them come to him but it was too late now.

Ben waved away the offer of a drink from the barman and kept his concentration on the stranger and Ackroyd.

When the man turned to face him Ben braced himself, ready to draw his weapon, but when he saw the man's face he realized that whoever was buried in Harpers Post it wasn't his brother. He could have been looking at himself when he was the same age as Lyle was now.

Lyle's eyes narrowed as he studied Ben.

'I've been waiting for you, Deputy.'

Whatever Lyle had on his mind it wasn't friendly or brotherly and he showed no sign of having recognized Ben.

'You don't know who I am, do you?' Ben asked.

'I know that you're the man who killed my friend Errol Carlisle and that's all I need to know about you,' replied Lyle. He stepped away from the bar but stayed facing Ben.

'Lyle, I'm your brother, Ben, and before you go for that gun we need to talk about our ma's death.'

Lyle frowned as Ben's words registered.

'Our ma! What are you talking about?

And my brother Ben's in prison. I don't know what your game is, mister.'

'I've told you, Lyle. I'm your brother and that's the truth.'

Lyle felt uneasy because this wasn't going according to plan and he wasn't sure how to handle it. He had come to shoot the deputy and now he was confused. The barman interrupted the silence as the brothers stared at each other.

'He's telling the truth, Lyle. He's your brother Ben and your ma's dead.'

'Look, I don't know what's happening here. I've come here to kill you because Kelvin Carlisle paid me to, but if you're my brother I ain't going to do that. What happened to Ma? She's too young to be dead. She wasn't ever sick.'

Ben could see that Lyle was spooked but at least the threat of confrontation had eased for the moment and he decided to take matters slowly.

'Why don't we walk over to the marshal's office, Lyle, and talk things through. I promise that no one will harm you. But you know that you're going to have to pay for those other things that you've done.'

Lyle's mood changed as he snapped back at Ben.

'What things! I've never killed anyone. I suppose you think I did because they were aiming to hang me. Well I didn't and I'm not going to be arrested. Not by you and not by the marshal.'

Ben realized that he hadn't taken things as slowly as he'd planned and needed to calm things down.

'I'm only interested in what happened to Ma. It seems that you were the last person to see her before she was murdered at the house. But what you just said doesn't make sense because you confessed to killing a man and were going to hang for it, and what about the man who was killed during your escape?'

'I'm telling you, I'm no killer. Not Ma, for Christ's sake, or Joe Spence, and I don't know anything about Jeb Doran. He was alive when I left the marshal's office. Errol Carlisle killed Joe Spence and I agreed to take the blame.'

Ben was still anxious to hear about his mother and pressed his brother.

'So when was the last time that you saw Ma?'

'The night that Errol broke me out of jail,' Lyle replied. 'We went to see her at the house and I tried to talk her into selling up to Kelvin Carlisle. She wouldn't listen and we had a big row and we left. When we got outside Errol said he was going back in to try and see if she would listen to him, but he came back out and said that Ma still wouldn't change her mind. The Carlisles have been hiding me on their ranch ever since because I'd agreed to take the blame when Errol killed Joe Spence. It was arranged that they would help me escape and old man Carlisle would pay me for my trouble. And I mean pay me, like big time.'

Ben believed Lyle's story because it all fitted together.

'So Errol must have killed Ma,' Ben reasoned. 'I was right about him after all. No wonder he didn't want Clarissa around him. If you're innocent, Lyle, then give yourself up now.'

Lyle shook his head. 'No chance. It would be my word against Kelvin Carlisle's and he could buy his way out of anything. I'm not sure if he knows about Errol killing Ma but he knows about the rest of it. No, I'm leaving now and I don't think you'll stop me, brother. When Clarissa's a bit older, tell her that I was sorry and explain everything to her.'

Lyle gave his brother a weak smile and walked away, leaving Ben with the biggest decision of his life. Had his brother just told him a pack of lies, even though it all made sense? By the time Ben had reached his decision and drawn his pistol from the holster Lyle had stepped through the swing doors of the saloon. Lyle was reaching for the reins of his horse by the time that Ben called out to him.

'Lyle, don't make me shoot. If you mount that horse you'll leave me no choice.'

Lyle placed his left foot in the stirrup and turned towards Ben who was pointing his gun at him.

'Do what you have to do, brother. So long, Ben.'

The first bullet ripped into Lyle's shoulder, the second into his chest as he fell back on to the bottom step of the saloon. The men who had been playing cards ran out of the saloon and gawked down at Lyle, watching the blood pump from his body in little spurts. A sweaty little character with a pencil-thin moustache turned to one of his playing partners.

'That's ten dollars you owe me. I just knew he'd plug him. Brother or no brother.'

Ben looked across the street and saw Bob Doran throw the still-smouldering rifle into the street, raise his arms above his head and walk towards the mar-shal's office. He had just sentenced himself to a date with the noose for killing the man he had wrongly suspected of killing his son Jeb and now he would never avenge his son's death.

Ben threw his own gun aside, knelt down on the steps and cradled his dying brother's head in his arms. Lyle gave him a faint smile and his eyes were only half-open as he asked:

'You wouldn't have shot me, would you, Ben?'

Ben swallowed hard. 'No, I wouldn't have shot you, Lyle, and that's the truth.'

'I've never killed anyone, Ben, and that's the truth as well.'

Ben hugged his brother's bloodied body as he replied, 'I know, brother, I know.'

He hoped that Lyle had heard because his brother never spoke another word.

★   ★   ★

A small group had gathered around the steps of the saloon, including William Connor, who untied a blanket from

Lyle's horse and covered his body. Ben wiped the tears from his eyes before picking up his gun and running back into the saloon but not before he had ordered the vultures to go about their business. Sol Ackroyd was on his way out of the saloon when he was sent crashing to the floor by the blow from the butt of Ben's pistol.

Ben straddled the semiconscious Ackroyd and placed his gun under the man's bloodied nostrils and cocked the weapon.

'Now I want you to tell me exactly what the Carlisles have been up to and if I have the slightest doubt that you are not telling me all that you know then I'll kill you. Now start talking.'

Ackroyd talked, knowing full well that his life depended on it. Errol Carlisle had shot Joe Spence over a stupid argument. Lyle had been with him at the time playing cards in a private room at the back of the Drinking Well but other people had known that they were there. Errol and

Lyle rode out to the Carlisle ranch and told Kelvin Carlisle what had happened. Errol wanted his father to give him money so that he could escape hanging by going to Mexico. It was then that Kelvin Carlisle offered Lyle a large sum of money if he would take the blame. Kelvin would arrange his escape and hide him on the ranch until everything went quiet. Under Kelvin's orders, Ackroyd had arranged for a decoy to act as Lyle. He was meant to keep on travelling but he had stayed in Harpers Post, where Ben nearly caught up with him. Ackroyd was there when Lyle escaped but claimed that Errol shot Jeb Doran because he thought he had recognized him. Lyle was outside at the time and they told him that they had just fired a shot to scare Jeb. Ackroyd was with Errol one night when they were both really drunk and Errol started rambling. It was then that he confessed that he'd strangled Evelyn Gleeson. Kelvin Carlisle had said in front of his son that he wished Ma

Gleason was dead and Errol probably thought his father would be pleased.

'And that's all I know except that it was Errol who set fire to the marshal's office when you were in the cell. The only reason that he raised the alarm and helped rescue you was because he thought he'd been seen by someone when he was carrying some straw in.'

'Right, now get up,' Ben ordered. 'I'm going to lock you up and then I'm going after Carlisle. You'll be having him for a cell mate if I can stop myself from killing him.'

★   ★   ★

Ben rode out to the Carlisle ranch feeling the same anger as when he had run across the street all those years ago, after he had heard that his father had been attacked. He was going to see a man whose greed for power had caused so much misery. Arberstown might have prospered under Carlisle but it would be a better place without him. The one thing that he couldn't understand was why Carlisle hadn't arranged to have Lyle killed, because he would have been aware that Lyle could have incriminated him at any time. Ben would never know that Lyle had safeguarded his position through some sort of legal arrangement.

The large gate to the Carlisle property was closed. One of the two guards stepped in front of Ben's horse and asked him what his business was.

'Marshal Brewster left instructions for me to deliver an important message to Mr Carlisle,' Ben lied, hoping to trick his way in.

The men opened the gate and waved him through and he started on the long trail that led to the Carlisle house. He couldn't help but note the spectacular scenery despite the seriousness of what had brought him here. One thing for sure; God never intended it to belong to one man, not even a good man, let alone someone like Kelvin Carlisle. He was still some distance away when he saw the Carlisle house for the first time. It looked more like a government building with its colonial-style pillars that soared higher than any building he had ever seen even on his visits back East.

When he eventually neared the entrance to the house a huge black man stepped forward and steadied his horse as he dismounted.

'Massa Carlisle is expecting you, Mr Gleason. I'll arrange for your animal to be groomed while you are in the house.'

Ben thanked the man, but was puzzled how his arrival could have been expected unless the men who had stopped him at the entrance had used some sort of signalling system. Before his outstretched hand reached the brightly polished brass door-handle, the giant oak door opened and he was ushered in by another equally large black servant. The man asked Ben if he could take his gun belt but it seemed more of a request than a demand and Ben gave him an equally polite 'No thanks'.

Stepping into the large oak panelled drawing-room he was relieved to see that Marshal Brewster was there, hoping that it might just make things easier. Ben wasn't sure what sort of reception he would get from Carlisle but he was soon left in no doubt.

'I never thought that I would see the day when my son's killer would enter this house.' The words were spat out by Carlisle who was sitting behind his desk. Carlisle's face didn't just show the scars of his recent loss but those of a man who had been unhappy with the world for a long time. If Ben had his way he would soon be put out of his misery.

Carlisle was clearly made nervous by Ben's presence and he looked anxiously towards the marshal, who was seated near the desk.

'What's all this about, Ben?' asked the marshal. 'Why are you here? I was just about to head back to town. What's happened?'

Ben laughed. 'Nothing much, Marshal. I've just come to arrest this little runt for conspiracy to murder.'

The marshal tried to calm things. 'I don't know what's brought this on, Ben, but perhaps we'd better go back to town and talk this through. Then I'll decide what to do.'

Kelvin Carlisle had regained his composure and seemed amused by Ben's accusation.

'How is your brother?' he asked. 'Still alive and well I hope.'

'My brother's dead, but unlike your weasel of a son, he didn't deserve to die.'

Carlisle frowned and clenched his fist. He moved his hand towards the right hand-drawer of his desk but withdrew it quickly and placed it back on the desk.

Carlisle sneered once more. 'So you have killed your brother and now you come here with some ludicrous accusations to make you feel better. What sort of man kills his own brother, even in the name of the law?'

'I didn't kill my brother, but I expect

the marshal is wondering why you assumed that I had. Well, we both know it's because you sent him into town today to do your dirty work.'

Marshal Brewster was looking uncomfortable as he addressed Ben.

'All this is pretty strong stuff, Ben. What sort of proof do you have?'

'For starters, this creature's son, Errol, strangled my mother just to please his daddy. Don't worry, I've got proof. Sol Ackroyd is locked in one of the cells and he's willing to sing like a bird. So, are you going to arrest this snake, Marshal, or will you give me the pleasure, but I'm not leaving here without him!'

Marshal Brewster stood up and pointed his gun at Carlisle before directing it towards Ben.

'I'm sorry, I can't do that, Ben. The moment you rode through those gates you signed your own death warrant. Now unbuckle your belt and place it on Mr Carlisle's desk. Don't make me be the one to kill you, Ben.'

Ben shook his head as he unbuckled the belt and followed the marshal's instructions.

'Not you, Marshal,' Ben groaned with disappointment and disbelief. 'I thought you hated him just like everyone else. How long have you been taking his money? Just tell me that.'

'If it makes you feel any better, just an hour ago. The thing is, Ben, you would have died with or without my involvement. Mr Carlisle has offered me a comfortable retirement and I feel that I've earned it.'

'Blood-money won't bring you any comfort, Marshal. Let's go and get this over with.' Ben leaned towards the desk once more and smiled at Carlisle. 'You'll end up in hell one day, little man, and your cowardly son will be waiting to greet you.'

Ben was pleased that he had inflicted some further discomfort on Kelvin Carlisle as he saw his eye twitch and the face flush with rage.

When Ben reached the door Carlisle

had managed to control himself.

'Good bye, Mr Gleason,' he called. 'I'm sorry that all your hard work on the house was wasted. I expect to acquire the Gleason land when all the legalities are completed in a few weeks. Oh, and I may try to adopt your sweet little sister.'

Ben froze but the increased pressure of Brewster's gun in his back reminded him of the futility of attempting anything dramatic. He wouldn't give Carlisle the added pleasure of seeing him die. He concluded that everything must have been prearranged because their horses were waiting outside the house, but there was no sign of the servants who had welcomed him to the great mansion just a short time ago. Ben climbed into the saddle wondering what the next move would be.

'Don't try anything stupid, Ben,' Marshal Brewster said in a low voice, 'and I might just be able to get you out of this alive. I've been told to hand you over just outside the main grounds. I'm not about to join Carlisle's payroll despite what was said in there. I'll explain everything later. That's if we get out of this alive.'

Ben was thinking that he couldn't see why the marshal would need to lie to him unless it was just a ploy to get him to co-operate and then he saw the glint on the barrel of the rifle on the roof of the stables opposite. The shot hit the marshal in his forehead and Ben's horse reared, frightened by the sound, and caused the shot intended for Ben to thud into the animal's neck. He fell heavily as the horse crumpled to the ground. The third shot was hurried, causing the bullet to hit the brickwork beside the door, allowing Ben to scamper inside. There was no smile on the servant's face this time as he advanced towards Ben. Ben just managed to grab the heavy coat-stand near the door and ram the base of it into the servant's face, causing him to drop in his tracks, out cold.

Kelvin Carlisle was fumbling for the

gun in the desk drawer but Ben had reached his own gun which was still on the desk. He brandished it close to the terrified Carlisle's face.

'Now take your hand away and put it on the desk or I'll end this for you right here and now,' Ben threatened.

'You still won't leave my land alive,' said Carlisle, returning Ben's threat.

'If I don't, then neither will you. Now get up, you little snake,' Ben ordered, 'and come to the front of the desk and make it quick.'

Carlisle whimpered when Ben placed the gun against his ear and cocked the weapon.

'I'll set you up for life. You will be able to live anywhere you want in luxury, but please don't kill me,' Carlisle pleaded.

'Open your mouth and do exactly like I say and you might live long enough to face a hanging.'

Carlisle hesitated, so Ben forced the barrel inside Carlisle's mouth, causing a front tooth to chip and his lip to bleed.

Following Ben's instructions they edged their way towards the front door and passed the servant who was still lying on the floor groaning.

He wasn't surprised to see the group of armed men positioned on the other side of the courtyard.

'Mr Carlisle wants you to throw away your weapons and lie face down on the ground,' he shouted at them. 'Isn't that right, Mr Carlisle?'

Carlisle was further angered by the mocking tone in Ben's orders but he nodded in agreement. The men kept their weapons pointing towards Ben, uncertain what their next move should be, but after a second threat by Ben one of them threw down his weapon and the other two followed his lead.

Ben waited until they were all lying face down and he was sure that no one else was lurking in the vicinity of the house, then he ordered Carlisle to mount the marshal's horse.

Once Ben had climbed up behind Carlisle he held the gun against the back of Carlisle's head and ordered him to ride to town. But Ben was remembering the guards at the entrance to the property and was worried that he might not even get off Carlisle land. The ride to the main gate was slow and Ben was still anxious as he ordered Carlisle to pull up the horse just short of the gate. The two guards followed Ben's order to open the gate and seemed rather bemused by the fate of Carlisle. Ben didn't expect them to follow him into town.

The sight of Ben and Carlisle riding down Main Street caused a stir amongst those watching and word quickly spread about their arrival. By the time that Ben had dragged Carlisle off the horse, a small crowd had gathered outside the jail. Some of the townsfolk had never seen their landlord before and one quipped:

'Is that the little runt who's been bleeding us dry all these years?'

Others joined in and even though they did not realize the full significance of Carlisle's capture there was almost a sense of the town being liberated and there were cries of 'Well done, Ben'.

After Ben had secured his prisoner he asked Walter Kearney to look after things while he went to see William Connor and told him what had happened. Connor listened in disbelief before leaving his house with Ben to go and convene an emergency meeting of the town's leading figures.

During the meeting Ben was appointed acting marshal and John Neville was instructed to send for Judge Jardine to conduct Carlisle's trial. It was agreed that Sol Ackroyd would be released on the condition that he sorted things out at the Carlisle ranch. Ackroyd would be ordered to sack those who would be likely to cause trouble and to warn those who might be tempted to rescue Carlisle that they would be shot on sight.

Ben didn't like Ackroyd but there was no evidence to link him with any of the serious crimes attributed to Carlisle so it seemed sensible to make use of him, or so he thought.

★　★　★

On the night before Carlisle's trial Ben visited the cell. Carlisle seemed angry and agitated. He had shown a remarkable calm and a degree of arrogance in recent days and Ben had begun to wonder if his legal people might have nobbled Judge Jardine. In contrast to Carlisle's demeanour, many of the townsfolk had become anxious that he might escape punishment and their feeling of liberation had ebbed in recent days. Some of those who had rejoiced and openly insulted their tyrant landlord had become worried that he would have his revenge if he managed to worm his way out of the charges. Ackroyd had told Ben that Carlisle had never actually killed anyone and that he had made sure that others had done his dirty work. Ben was having second thoughts about the decision to use Ackroyd because that might discredit him as the key witness. Carlisle's lawyer might claim that Ackroyd had fabricated the stories about Carlisle in order to save his own skin. The main plank of Carlisle's defence was that the horrible deeds that he was accused of had been done by others who thought they might please him. Some of them had overstepped the mark, including his son.

Ben had being staying at the Connors' when he wasn't on duty, for fear that Mary Jane and Clarissa might be endangered in some way in order to get back at him. He realized that he was probably being paranoid but he feared that Carlisle could use his wealth in so many different ways to escape the punishment he deserved, the death penalty.

Ben had only just managed to bed down on the sofa and drift into sleep after thinking about tomorrow's trial when the hammering on the Connors' front door woke him up.

When Ben opened the door, Tommy Smail, one of the part-time barmen from the Drinking Well tried to get the words out but he was still breathless from running.

'Deputy, er, Marshal, you'd better come quick. There's been some shooting at the jail.'

Ben didn't wait to hear any more. He ran back inside to collect his gun belt, then ran towards the marshal's office, leaving the out-of-condition Tommy Smail coughing outside the Connors' house.

'Damn, damn. I knew it would happen.' Ben cursed himself as he ran. Why hadn't he stayed at the jailhouse last night? He could have asked someone to look after Mary Jane and Clarissa.

Despite it being the early hours of the morning a small crowd was gathered outside the marshal's office, mostly late night drinkers from the saloon. He had to push his way through them.

'What's happened here, Marshal?'

someone shouted.

Ben rattled the office door after finding it locked. He was relieved to find that it was opened by an unharmed Walter Kearney, who had been on night duty.

'How did it happen, Walter?' Ben asked as he glanced towards the open door of Carlisle's cell.

'I swear I just don't know,' Walter replied.

'At least whoever freed him didn't harm you.'

Ben had walked towards the cell and he didn't hear Walter say:

'Didn't Tommy tell you what happened?' Carlisle's brains were splattered inside the cell. A gun lay on the floor beside the body.

Ben felt no sadness at Carlisle's death but he had a duty to find out how it had happened and that would mean questioning Walter Kearney. Although it was never proven, it was generally felt that Carlisle's men had been responsible for the death of Jack Kearney, and if so,

Walter had good reason for seeing Carlisle die. Walter had been amongst those who had expressed their concern that Carlisle would somehow escape punishment.

Ben had no doubt that Walter was an honest man at heart, built in the mould of his father, but there was something that Ben needed to know.

'Walter, it pains me to ask, but did you have anything to do with this?'

Walter wasn't offended by his friend's question. If he didn't ask it, others would. He looked Ben in the eye as he replied:

'I swear on my pa's memory that I didn't, Ben.'

Ben offered his hand to his big friend, signifying that the matter was closed.

★   ★   ★

Several days after Carlisle's death Ben heard that Carlisle had made extraordinary last minute changes to his will.

The day before he died Carlisle had written a new will in which he left all his land to be used as a national park and the house was bequeathed to the people of Arberstown.

Perhaps Carlisle couldn't face the humiliation of a trial, or he had reflected on his evil doings and was remorseful. Ben never found out for certain who smuggled the gun to Carlisle but the chief suspect was a woman who had visited Carlisle, claiming that she was part of his legal team. Whoever it was it looked as though Carlisle's money got him what he wanted, right to the end.

# 15

When Ben and Mary Jane announced their engagement it was with the blessing of William Connor. Connor had come to realize that his strict ways had almost committed his daughter to a life of misery. He had been hard on Ben, forgetting that he had been young at the time and perhaps he might have been the sort of man who could not have lived with himself had he not avenged his father. Arberstown had a lot to thank Ben for and Connor knew that he would look after Mary Jane.

Ben had agreed to stay on as marshal, but only until the town could appoint someone else. Ben believed that Marshal Brewster had intended to dupe Carlisle in order to uncover his shady operations. Marshal Brewster had been a fine servant of Arberstown and would be a difficult man to replace. Ben had been honoured when the town council had presented him with the marshal's fine pearl handled pistol but he had no plans to be a full-time lawman.

Within four months of the Gleason house being destroyed by fire the new ranch house had been built just a short distance away from the original one, thanks to the hard work of Ben and Walter Kearney. It wasn't the mansion that Ben planned to build one day. That would take time but for now the new home would be suitable for him and Clarissa and in a few months, Mary Jane when she became his wife.

The town council had been contacted by the legal people and it looked as though they were going to get their businesses back. Arberstown was once again a happy place. The Carlisle property was now being looked after by an administrator and Sol Ackroyd had been told that he was no longer required. He had been dismissed with a paltry pay-off after years of doing Carlisle's dirty work but he didn't blame Carlisle. He still had a strange loyalty towards the man even though he would have testified against him to save his own skin. Ben Gleason was the man to blame for his current misfortune. If Gleason hadn't come back things would have stayed just as they were but everything had gone wrong ever since Gleason had turned up. And Ackroyd wasn't forgetting the beating that Gleason had given him the day that Lyle was killed.

Ackroyd had decided to leave Arberstown and had just paid his last visit to the Drinking Well saloon when he saw the pony and carriage with Mary Jane Connor and the little Gleason girl on board. Mary Jane called out to her mother who was outside the store and told her that they were going to the Gleason ranch. She also mentioned that Ben was on duty all afternoon over at the marshal's office.

The chance conversation made Ackroyd decide he would call at the Gleason place and say a proper goodbye to Mary Jane. She looked more womanly than ever. She certainly had a new confidence and sparkle about her. Perhaps Gleason hadn't waited for their wedding night and had been pleasuring himself on her already. Well if Gleason could put a smile on her face then Ackroyd could as well. He'd never had any complaints from the saloon girls. Perhaps he might be able to sweet talk her but he would have to get that little Gleason girlie out of the way first. And if the gorgeous Mary Jane didn't want to oblige him then he would have to carry out what old man Carlisle had once suggested, and just take her. Afterwards he would lie low in the cabin where Lyle had gone into hiding until things quietened down and then he would move on.

★   ★   ★

Ben had spotted Mary Jane and Clarissa ride past his office half an hour earlier when Walter Kearney called in and mentioned that he had seen Ackroyd riding towards the Gleason ranch.

'He was riding at a fair gallop on Lyle's black stallion and I didn't get the impression that he was out for an afternoon ride. Did you send him out there?'

Ben shook his head. 'I haven't spoken to him for weeks because he tends to stay clear of me and I'm glad about that.' Ben didn't trust Ackroyd and reached for his hat. 'I'm going out to the house, Walter. Mary Jane and Clarissa will be there by now and I'll feel better if I go and check things out. Thanks for letting me know. Ackroyd might have just ridden by the house but he's been drinking very heavily these past weeks.'

⋆   ⋆   ⋆

Ackroyd felt a strange sort of excitement as he neared the Gleason house and spotted the carriage outside. He hadn't done anything like this before and he guessed that was the reason for how he was feeling. It was a little bit like he felt after he had shot Jeb Doran when helping Errol to break Lyle out of jail. If he had left it to feeble Errol he would be in prison now or even worse. Ackroyd smiled, wondering how Gleason would have felt knowing that he was indirectly to blame for getting Lyle shot. Poor Lyle had got himself killed without really doing anything wrong, except for being a greedy little nobody.

Ackroyd was tying the stallion to the hitch rail outside the house when Mary Jane and Clarissa came out. They didn't see the sneer on Ackroyd's face as he glanced over at the charred building that he had helped set on fire.

'Hello, Mr Ackroyd,' said Mary Jane, greeting him with a friendly smile. 'If you've come to see Ben, he's at the marshal's office.'

'That's a shame. I was told he was working up here. I wanted to talk business with him,' Ackroyd lied. 'Ah well, I'll just have to ride back to town to see him, but I sure would appreciate a glass of water. It's so damned hot today.'

'I've got some lemonade inside if you would prefer it. I made it for Clarissa but I'm sure she won't mind if you have some.'

Ackroyd gave a forced smile in return. He had noticed Clarissa taking an interest in the stallion.

'Isn't he a beauty, miss? Your brother was a fine judge of horses and I'm going to take special care of him. The thing is, he doesn't like being alone. Do you think you could keep him company while I go and have some of your lemonade? I promise I won't drink it all.'

Clarissa replied with a shy 'Yes' and sat down on the steps of the porch close to the horse.

Mary Jane was surprised when Ackroyd came inside the house and followed her across the room to where the container of lemonade was. She felt uncomfortable at his closeness as she poured the drink. So close that she could smell the alcohol on his breath. She was used to men giving her admiring glances, particularly during recent months, but Ackroyd was not just looking at her body, he was studying it as though he was undressing her in his mind.

'I think we had better go and join Clarissa on the porch. I'll take her some lemonade,' said Mary Jane, eager to get outside and avoid the prying eyes of Ackroyd who was now sweating heavily.

'Let her be a little while. She's enjoying that fine horse of mine. I never did get a proper chance to speak to you, Mary Jane, and I'm leaving Arberstown for good today.'

'What was it you wanted to see Ben about?' she asked.

'Ben!' Ackroyd exclaimed. 'I don't want to see Gleason. That was just an excuse to see you before I go. Gleason's a lucky man and I'm sure he won't mind me calling in to say farewell to the finest looking woman in Arberstown, and for miles around if I'm not mistaken.'

Mary Jane was not just feeling uncomfortable, she was now very frightened.

'I think you'd better leave, Mr Ackroyd. Ben will be here soon and I don't think he would be very pleased if he found you here. Just leave now and I promise I will say you just called in to let Clarissa see Lyle's horse.'

'Now come on, Mary Jane, relax. You ain't married yet. Why don't we just drift along to the bedroom and have a bit of fun. Once you're hitched you'll be stuck with the same man until you die, always wondering how different it might be with another man. Where's the harm? I promise you all men are not the same, if you know what I mean.'

Any doubt that Mary Jane had about Ackroyd's intentions had now gone and she headed towards the door. To her surprise he didn't follow, but called after her.

'I think that little girl would be safer if you stayed here, don't you?' The threat was clear and it stopped Mary Jane in her tracks.

'If I give you what you want, will you leave her alone?' Mary Jane pleaded.

'Look lady, I've just come here for a bit of pleasure and that's all. It's no big deal and I think you'll enjoy yourself. But I aim to get what I came for one way or the other and if someone gets hurt then that's down to you.'

Mary Jane had to play for time and hope she could get herself out of this nightmare but first she must try and safeguard Clarissa.

'Let me take Clarissa a drink and tell her to stay and look after your horse. We don't want her coming in and finding us . . . ' Mary Jane felt sickened at the thought. 'You can watch me from the window.'

'Sure you can, but don't say I didn't warn you if I catch you trying something.'

Mary Jane's hands were shaking as

she poured the lemonade for Clarissa and took it out on to the porch.

Clarissa seemed absorbed by the horse as she took the drink from Mary Jane and started drinking it without taking her gaze off the animal.

Mary Jane tried to calm herself as she told Clarissa to finish her drink and then run away from the house and hide in the woods. She explained that the man in the house wasn't very nice but she would be safe in the woods.

Once back inside the house, Mary Jane frantically tried to think how she could persuade Ackroyd not to carry out what he had come to do. She pleaded with him to ride away, and tried to make him believe that she wouldn't tell anyone that he had been there.

He reacted angrily to her suggestion. 'Look, we made a deal and there's not going to be any discussion. Now we can do it here or make ourselves more comfortable. I don't mind which as long as we get on with it. What's it going to be?'

* ★ ★

Ben's worst fears were confirmed when
he saw Clarissa running towards the
woods. Mary Jane wouldn't let her run
off by herself, not even here on their
property. He pulled on the reins and
steered his mount in the direction of
Clarissa. His shouts to her were ignored
until he got closer and she realized that
it was him. He dismounted before the
horse had stopped and hugged his
frightened sister. She sobbed as she
explained about Mary Jane's instructions and about the man in the house.

'Now you just stay here, honey, and
I'll be back soon, I promise.'

Ben mounted his horse and heeled it
into motion, galloping off towards the
house, fearful about what was happening inside.

He dismounted alongside Ackroyd's
horse, jumped on to the porchway and
then burst through the front door with
no plan in mind except to grab Ackroyd.

Ackroyd had his back to the door as

he faced the terrified Mary Jane, who was the other side of the table. The pretty dress had been ripped from the shoulder and she looked terrified. Ackroyd seemed so preoccupied with trying to reach her that he had not heard Ben enter the room. It was the look of relief on Mary Jane's face as she looked over Ackroyd's shoulder that caused him to turn around and then see the advancing figure of Ben.

Although taken by surprise, Ackroyd was the first to draw his gun. If Mary Jane hadn't pushed the table against him the bullet would have hit Ben and not embedded itself in the wall behind him.

Ben shot into Ackroyd's chest, knocking him back against the table before he pitched forward and lay on his side. Ben kicked Ackroyd's gun away. He then used his boot to push Ackroyd on to his back. He checked that the man was dead before he hugged Mary Jane and smothered her with kisses. When he tried to release her, she gripped him, her body trembling as the shock took effect.

'I didn't let him, Ben. I didn't let him, I didn't let him,' she repeated between sobs.

'I know, Mary Jane, you're one brave lady and you saved my life as well. Now let's get something to cover you and we'll go and get Clarissa. She's waiting over by the woods.'

'Thank God you came out here. It's a miracle.'

'It might be so, Mary Jane, but we have Walter Kearney to thank as well because he told me about Ackroyd heading this way.'

Later that night Mary Jane told Ben that Ackroyd had mentioned that he was the one who had shot Jeb Doran and that he was glad that Lyle had got the blame for it. It pleased Ben that in some way he had avenged his brother's death by killing Ackroyd. The following day Ben told the town council that he no longer wished to be temporary marshal because he was bringing his wedding plans forward.

# 16

It was almost three years after Ben had ridden off the Carlisle property following the arrest of Kelvin Carlisle before he visited it again. There were no guards this time as he guided the wagon up the long trail towards the house. His wife Mary Jane sat beside him and Clarissa was in the back seat playing with her baby nephew, William. Behind them there was a long snake of wagons that contained almost the entire population of Arberstown. When the mansion came into sight Clarissa leaned forward.

'Is that it, Ben? Is that the hospital?'

'That's it, honey. That's the Evelyn Gleason Hospital,' Ben replied with pride.

Mary Jane's eyes misted as she squeezed her husband's arm, knowing what today meant to him.

There had been a large influx of

people into Arberstown and the surrounding area in recent years and it had been decided to turn the house into a hospital. As a reward to Ben for freeing the town of Carlisle the council had chosen to name the hospital after his mother.

The people of Arberstown had mixed views on why Carlisle had bequeathed the house to the town. Some saw it as a remorseful act of someone who had seen the light. Others believed that he might have thought he could buy his way into heaven. The answer could have been provided by the lady who had joined the crowds visiting the park that day. Heather Carlisle had come to visit her son's grave. She had arranged that one day she would be laid to rest in the grave next to his, which already bore her name and contained a coffin filled with rocks that had been lowered there under the orders of Kelvin Carlisle.

When Heather had visited her husband in jail the day before he died, posing as a legal representative, he had thought that he was seeing a ghost. Despite the passing years she was still a beautiful woman and immediately recognizable.

Several weeks after Heather had been driven away from the Carlisle house within hours of Errol being born, Carlisle had received a letter from Sam Cameron. Cameron, who had worked for Carlisle, had been given the task of taking Heather Carlisle to Harpers Post and putting her on a train to start her journey East. In the letter Cameron said that Heather had died before reaching Harpers Post, from complications in connection with having just given birth. Carlisle had made it clear to his wife that unless she left she would be thrown out and left penniless. He had given her a generous sum of money to start a new life on the condition that she never returned or attempted to contact her son.

Carlisle's hopes of getting off the charges against him were shattered when his wife told him that she intended to testify against him. She had knowledge that would incriminate him in murders and other wrongdoings.

When Heather had heard about Carlisle's suicide and the changes to his will she knew that Carlisle had taken the coward's way out and that he had changed the will out of spite to prevent her inheriting his fortune. Heather Carlisle had no need of her late husband's money because she had built a successful business with Sam Cameron and was wealthy in her own right. She could have contested the will but settled for a legal guarantee that she would be buried next to her son one day. Heather Carlisle was an intelligent and resourceful woman who would have been an asset to her husband and her son if he had ever become governor of the state.

Ben Gleason was proud that his dear mother's name would live on for a long, long time after Kelvin Carlisle's had been forgotten.

We do hope that you have enjoyed reading this large print book.

Did you know that all of our titles are available for purchase?

We publish a wide range of high quality large print books including:
**Romances, Mysteries, Classics General Fiction Non Fiction and Westerns**

Special interest titles available in large print are:
**The Little Oxford Dictionary Music Book, Song Book Hymn Book, Service Book**

Also available from us courtesy of Oxford University Press:
**Young Readers' Dictionary (large print edition) Young Readers' Thesaurus (large print edition)**

For further information or a free brochure, please contact us at:
**Ulverscroft Large Print Books Ltd., The Green, Bradgate Road, Anstey, Leicester, LE7 7FU, England.
Tel:** (00 44) 0116 236 4325
**Fax:** (00 44) 0116 234 0205

*Other titles in the*
*Linford Western Library:*

# HONDO COUNTY GUNDOWN

## Chad Hammer

The Valley of the Wolf was no place for strangers, but Chet Beautel was not the usual breed of drifter. He was a straight-shooting man of the mountains searching for something better than what lay behind. Instead, he encountered a new brand of terror enshrouded in a mystery which held a thousand people hostage — until he saddled up to challenge it with a mountain man's grit and courage, backed up by a blazing .45. If Wolf Valley was ever to be peaceful again, Chet Beautel would be that peacemaker.